FLAT ON MY BACK

'One of the funniest bo

'Having eventua
Alida continues t
barassing illnesse
Germany, in-laws,
all like a slide on a … just
as hilarious.' – ANN

'A book we happily recommend.' – FORUM

'The domestic life of the Baxters is an hilarious double act that deserves star billing.'

– SMITH'S TRADE NEWS

Also by Alida Baxter

UP TO MY NECK
OUT ON MY EAR

FLAT ON MY BACK

Alida Baxter

A STAR BOOK

published by

the Paperback Division of

W. H. ALLEN & Co. Ltd.

A Star Book
Published in 1976
by the Paperback Division of
W. H. Allen & Co. Ltd.
A Howard & Wyndham Company
123 King Street, London W6 9JG

First published in Great Britain by
Michael Joseph Ltd.

Star edition reprinted 1977

Printed in Great Britain by
Richard Clay (The Chaucer Press), Ltd., Bungay, Suffolk

ISBN 0 352 39897 3

With much love to my poor family
and gratitude to Santa Claus.

Chapter One

I wouldn't be married at all, if it weren't for that stomach upset I had in 1969. I was run down, and being proposed to through the lavatory door caught me off my guard.

It all started when I met a Chartered Accountant, and I really should have known better. They're so wily they fill out Tax Returns for fun, like doing crossword puzzles, just to keep their hand in, and you must have seen them standing up and tramping out of thriller movies half an hour after the start, sighing with boredom; they've always worked out not only who's done it but who else is going to do it, and how, before anyone else in the audience has got the wrapper off their ice-cream.

There I was in my innocence, leading a happy life in Soho, spending my Saturday afternoons drinking free gin in the back of the Broadwick Street wine merchant's, gossiping with the white-haired gentlemen in the Algerian Coffee Stores, discussing mozzarella and olive oil pressings in Del Monico's, having friendly consultations with my gynaecologist and going out to dinner with men who didn't care how much I ate, when Wham! There was this Chartered Accountant. I'd met others before, of course, but I'd never been out with one. They're not a type you mix with socially in Soho. Men who manage bookshops, policemen, publicans, tailors, priests – yes. A.C.A.s – no. Unfamiliar though the breed was to me, we did seem to get on quite well, while we were at the polite stage, and we decided to go on holiday together that summer, to Spain. He behaved very strangely during the journey but I didn't find out why until much later, and after we landed I quickly forgot his airborne idiosyncracies because his behaviour on the ground riveted my attention. There were many things still to be learned about the members of his profession, one of them being their conservationist attitude to money.

From the first day of the holiday until the last, my boy friend carried around with him the same banknote for an astronomical quantity of pesetas, waving it at waiters and shopkeepers and taxi drivers and me, so that I dived for my own small change and went on diving until we got back to Heathrow. It was just one of the ploys I grew to know and admire. My companion was like the man with the million pound note; everybody trusted him, including me. But then, being incapacitated, I had no option.

Within forty-eight hours of our arrival, I'd gone down with a combination of Montezuma's Revenge and the Black Death. Useless in bed and too weak to climb out, I clamoured constantly for medical attention, and here the boy friend was only too willing to assist, but his efforts were hampered by a total lack of Spanish and the fact that we'd deliberately avoided going to an area where we were likely to be greeted with fluent Cockney or a Liverpudlian dialect.

'Haven't you found one yet?' I wailed plaintively from my truckle cot, when I was convinced he'd spent the afternoon painting a cross on the door. ' "*Medico*", I told you. "*Donde esta un medico*?" '

'There's only a chemist's,' he said glumly, 'with a French maniac behind the counter who wants to treat you himself. He says he saw you on the beach the first day, after you'd had all the rum and fallen off your deck-chair.'

'What did you tell him was wrong?' I fretted. 'Alcoholism?'

'I couldn't tell him, my French isn't good enough. I had to mime it.'

'You MIMED diarrhoea!'

My swain shifted about uncomfortably. 'It wasn't easy. He gave me an address but it turned out to be a midwife.'

'I'm dying,' I said flatly (and I was flat, for a change, what with no food and one thing and another), 'and I want a doctor.' If I'd trusted the strength of the bed, I would have had hysterics, but under the circumstances I controlled myself.

'How about a priest?' asked Old Helpful. 'There seem to be plenty of those.'

I groaned and turned my face to the wall. Of the two of us, why had cruel Fate immobilised the one who didn't care how badly she spoke three languages and left the perfectionist to roam around loose looking for somewhere to plug in his Linguaphone records?

A medico was eventually run to earth sitting in the baker's, but when he pranced into my bedroom and started unpacking his stethoscope the boy friend suddenly came over all British and possessive. The loquacious doctor gave me a thorough and appreciative examination (*such* a flattering activity and always guaranteed to cheer me up) but

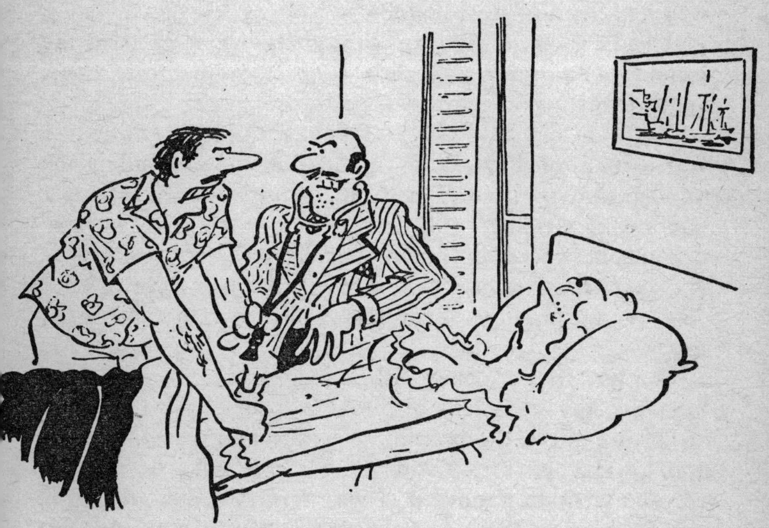

my compatriot insisted on remaining in the room the entire time, glowering suspiciously and occasionally stepping over and ostentatiously pulling down my nightie. At one point he was despatched to fetch a spoon, and was back with a ladle, panting, in three seconds, although the kitchen was at the other end of the flat. Personally I was thankful for that distance; the apartment belonged to English people and in their absence a colony of giant cockroaches had set up home under the sink. The articulated horrors were preparing for independence celebrations any day and I was determined to be out of the bed before they crawled into it.

'We don't need a ladle,' I snapped. 'El doctor only wants to look down my throat!'

The doctor flashed me the sort of smile that makes a speculum unnecessary, finished writing a lengthy prescription, asked whether I was insured and said he'd be back in a few days to see how I was progressing. When he'd gone I discovered it wasn't a prescription he'd been writing after all – it was a bill.

'Did he have to give you that going-over?' growled the jealous ladle-bearer, stomping back from the front door. 'You've got a stomach upset, not a prolapse.'

'What a churlish C.A.,' I thought, rather miffed. I was used to doctors taking one look at me and telling me to strip, having been a medical curiosity for years, and I had no idea that sort of thing would come as a surprise to someone who didn't know me very well.

'My G.P. gives me a D. and C. when I have a head cold,' I said proudly. 'That doctor seemed rather slap-dash to me.'

The boy friend looked disbelieving, but he made up for his unworthy suspicions by proving to be a great stalwart at carting me to the lavatory, fetching and carrying bowls and towels, and even taking off my eye make up when I was too weak to remove it (I was never too weak to put it on). I began to think he might be useful to have around, as a sort of ward orderly, and when I wasn't actually vomiting we did have some interesting talks. We had nothing in common, but that left us plenty of scope for discussion.

'It must be easy to divide the Spaniards into masochists and sadists,' I volunteered one day, from the echoing depths of the bathroom. (We conducted an incredible number of conversations with a door intervening.)

'How d'you mean?' came indistinctly from the outside world.

'The sadists manufacture the toilet paper and the masochists use it,' I said grimly.

I got through endless packets of Kleenex and set up my first record for the number of times I could block a loo in one day. For some reason foreign lavatories can't stomach paper handkerchiefs, and when he wasn't mopping my fevered brow or morosely counting unused contraceptives, my companion could usually be found wading about in the bathroom with his trousers rolled up and some long, drain-affiliated object in his hands, trying to free the pipes for the next onslaught. I never forgot the lesson I learned during those weeks, and conscientious Spanish Customs Officials had trouble controlling themselves when they found six-packs of Andrex in my cases during the years that followed.

There can't be all that many people who've received a proposal of marriage through a lavatory door and I sometimes consider ringing up the *Guinness Book of Records,* but perhaps an ex-nurse friend of mine has the edge on me. Her husband proposed to her after she'd given him an enema.

Our strange courtship survived a tour of Wales (where I had an imbalance of the inner ear and lived on Fernet Branca), a holiday in Portugal (where I went in the sea and had to be thawed with Triple Sec, and then nearly drowned in the shower because I was too drunk to find my way out), and all the preparations for our wedding. I'm not completely sure which of us called the whole thing off more often, but I think I won by a very short head. I also won the final pitched battle for the groom, but my head didn't have much to do with that.

For weeks before the wedding I was working up a froth baking the cakes, writing the invitations, destroying the evidence and generally not seeing much of my intended, and suddenly I realised that *he* was seeing altogether too much of his best man. The power cuts were on, but did they have to have all those candlelight dinners? And so what if I knew one hundred and sixty-eight enjoyable ways to risk a coronary? The competition had built-in contraception and carried a double sleeping bag around in case of emergencies.

I enrolled at a gymnasium and stopped playing hard to get, my underwear became so exciting that men at the office fought each other for the chance to stand behind me when I bent over the duplicating machine, and my legs nearly caused a collision at Oxford Circus, but all I did was to frighten my fiancé away. He said mournfully that I wasn't the girl he'd proposed to, but I couldn't stay in the lavatory for ever, and I was ploughing through Masters & Johnson for the nineteenth time when blessed inspiration stuck.

'Just try claiming a tax rebate for a chap,' I carolled, 'and see how far you get!' Gay Lib really should see about that loophole; it's one of the few advantages women have left.

So one December day we were married, in the middle of a power strike. Not what you'd call an auspicious omen. I remember that my husband nearly fractured my wrist trying to get the ring on my finger and because the Rector had given us a long talk on the symbolism of the ceremony I left the church feeling very pessimistic about the night to come. Things bucked up a bit at the reception, what with all the champagne, and apart from being caught showing my bridal garters to a waiter, and failing to prevent my friendly neighbourhood clairvoyant telling everybody the terrible truth about their year ahead, the afternoon went quite well. Something was bound to happen, of course, because receptions are like that, but when I slipped away to change and found my brand new husband lying on the floor of the Banqueting Manager's office, apparently dead, I was rather surprised. It's a chastening experience finding your husband dead when you don't know where he keeps his insurance policies. At first I thought the best man and I had killed him between us, but then I noticed the spot of blood.

My husband is usually so fit and well he's revolting, but he does suffer from what his mother describes as a known ailment she can't name. When she first told me this I thought syphilis, but she only meant he faints at the sight of his own blood; not my blood, or anybody else's blood, just his own. And he doesn't faint judiciously, he keels over like a felled pine wherever he happens to be when he starts to bleed, which is why we've got such deep carpet and underfelt in the bathroom. People who don't know about the felled pine routine think we experiment sexually and are scared of bruises.

When I'd got down on my hands and knees beside my groom and discovered the minute slit where he'd caught his thumb on the clasp of his going-away case, I began to wonder whether all the trouble had been worth it. Everyone except me was eating and drinking and throwing up and picking fights and making love to total strangers, and here was I with an unconscious Chartered Accountant and the Banqueting Manager's filing cabinets. And what was there to look forward to? After twenty-four hours of legalised sin in the Savoy I'd be setting up home in remote Pimlico, a distant outpost of Empire where even the bus numbers were unrecognisable. For me, London stopped south of Leicester Square. I'd lived in Soho all my life, in cold water flats with bathrooms and an aunt, cupboards without bathrooms or aunts and, latterly, a skyscraper with my mother, and I had deep misgivings about my new abode, a block where the porters wore uniforms like warders and even the prostitutes were middle class. Still, there'd be time enough to worry about that tomorrow;

my immediate problem was getting the groom up off the floor. I didn't like to ask anyone to come in and help me, because it would have looked so funny, but my husband's a big bloke and restoring him to a vertical position took so long that our dirty-minded friends gathered in the corridor and made loud remarks about our lack of control. Embarrassed, exhausted and fed up, I had the wording of my divorce petition off pat by the time we eventually emerged, and I only cheered up a little when someone threw an unopened bag of rice at my groom.

The rice thrower was given a warm hug, but I was somewhat reserved when saying goodbye to everyone else (it was hard, working out who would want what back when we announced our separation) and sat at attention in the taxi, strangling my fur hat, as we rattled along to the Savoy. Who could have known that staggered admiration was to defrost me within minutes of our arrival?

Precautions against the power cuts were in full swing and after a prideful description of the hotel's generator, a representative of the management led us to our room, assuring us that candelabra would be brought in if all else failed. 'The show must go on' was writ large on the faces of all the employees, and a war-time spirit positively thrummed through the corridors. Equally impervious to the bright goodwill all around him and the waves of ice emanating from me, the walking wounded took a look at the single beds, coughed and shed approximately three tons of confetti on the carpet.

'There seems to have been some mistake,' he said smoothly, putting an arm round my waist. 'This is our wedding night, and I hardly think . . .'

I was so flabbergasted I didn't even strike. What on earth was he playing at? I knew he'd phoned to book a twin-bedded room, in fact I'd insisted on it. For various reasons it's unnecessary to go into at the moment, I'd sooner share a bed with a Saint Bernard dog than my husband, and in fact . . .

But back at the Savoy the representative of the management had hot and cold running sweat and was practically grovelling. He got up off his knees to lead us to a suite and within minutes there were bouquets of roses burgeoning on every surface and telephoned assurances that in view of the hideous error there would be no extra charge for the living-room, or the television set, or the bar.

'How often have you done this before?' I stuttered, when we were alone, but my husband merely unravelled a complaisant smile and went to watch 'Some Like It Hot' on the colour T.V. As I lay on the bed listening to his complaints about the film being in black and white, I realised I had to hand it to him. Sometimes the sheer ingenuity of a Chartered Accountant achieves such heights it transcends criticism.

Chapter Two

Pimlico proved to be very strange indeed, but marriage was even stranger. The combination of marriage *and* Pimlico came as such a shock that I wondered whether it might actually be famous amongst mortals less insular than myself as a sort of tourist attraction, guaranteed to stimulate the blood, that people expected in S.W.1 when they couldn't drink the water.

The day after the wedding I went back home to visit my mother.

'Good God,' she said (it was a Sunday). 'What are you doing here?' It was obvious she thought she'd got rid of me; she'd been sitting with her feet up, wearing her cosiest slippers and loosest corsets, and had just baked herself a cake. Sunday papers sprawled everywhere and there was washing-up in the sink. I could see that whatever my marriage did to me, it suited her down to the ground.

I'd come to collect more clothes, because the heating in our flat was lying doggo in the basement refusing to crawl up the pipes, and my husband and I weren't on speaking terms, let alone prepared to warm each other up, but I said I wanted to borrow a corkscrew.

'Don't your neighbours use corkscrews?' asked my mother suspiciously.

'They're all very refined,' I bluffed. 'I think they must break the necks of bottles off against the walls.'

From bitter personal experience I would never recommend a honeymoon at home, particularly to anyone with a temper like mine or my husband's. If you're at home, when you slam out there is somewhere familiar and welcoming to go. You aren't in an intimidating foreign country, or on your best and most unnatural behaviour in an hotel, rowing in whispers and drinking heavily from nine a.m. onwards; you're probably near shops, cinemas and restaurants or, even worse, your families, and the temptation to leave the other faction stewing while you browse around Woolworth's is almost irresistible. If we hadn't been living at what seemed to parochial me like a bush station in the outback I doubt whether I'd have stayed around long enough to consummate the marriage, but it's amazing what boredom and cold weather can drive you to. Unfortunately keeping up the good work proved to be harder than I'd expected, and within days I knew God really didn't like me. I couldn't sit down and I wouldn't lie down and after much bitter complaint and threats of legal action my frustrated husband dragged me off to a woman doctor (his choice) who squinted up my orifices and said I had thrush. I'd thought thrush was something babies suffered from, in their mouths, but my soulmate was so pleased to hear I didn't have anything permanent, like frigidity, that he sang all the way home in the car and forgot to mark the bottle when I had my evening gin. We soon learned that it wasn't that simple. The treatment prescribed with warped menopausal humour for what was diagnosed as a reaction to the Pill necessitated not only celibacy but double-jointedness on my part, as I had to stand on my head and paint my nether regions with gentian violet four times a day. This artistic operation took hours to complete, had no effect on the thrush, did nothing to satiate our lust, and increased tension to the point where my husband stopped kicking the furniture and started kicking me instead. Despite being an animal lover, he said for some reason he had no qualms about maltreating a baboon.

Standing around glowering at my redundant mate only added to the attractions of the great outdoors and in spite of the prevailing conditions, which were that my husband wouldn't drive me anywhere in case I dyed the car seats and I had to walk because none of the buses in Pimlico went anywhere interesting, I managed to get fairly far afield. I even found that you could walk from Pimlico to Soho, though you flagged a bit coming up Lower Regent Street, and when I went back to work everyone commented on my beautifully developed calf muscles.

In due course my spouse also returned to his office and the usual filthy remarks in the humiliating knowledge that he'd had less to do with me after the wedding than before. I sometimes think he's been trying to make up for it ever since.

We'd married ten days before Christmas and in early December had fought our way to the crowded counters to spend large quantities of money on apparent essentials like musk and transparent underwear, and it wasn't until

my husband had humped me over the threshold and started bellowing for food and drink that we realised we'd each thought the other would provide the housekeeping until our next pay day. We were turning away three cross parties of carol singers a day and were down to corn-flakes and Russian tea when my boss caught telepathy and saved the situation by sending me my bonus in cash in a registered envelope. My husband tore open the famine relief with trembling fingers, having beaten me away with his umbrella, and I smouldered at him from a corner, plotting dreadful revenge once my thrush had cleared up.

'Just remember,' he'd whispered gently as we walked down the aisle, 'that bit about "those whom Thou by Matrimony hadst made one"? Well, I'm the one.'

As I watched him counting my bonus and murmuring 'Steak, fillet steak,' with saliva at the corners of his mouth, I had to admit that at least he was honest to a fault.

Considering our joint income took us into the Surtax bracket, I could never understand why time went by and we continued to be so short of money. There were whole dry and acrimonious week-ends when neither of us had the wherewithal for a bottle of tonic wine, and even now we're still at the 'Let's forget Christmas this year' stage, always promising to buy presents and never going out to get them. This is a pity because my husband is present-mad. He loves buying himself little gifts and rushing home to show me his latest treasure, his rosy face shining with child-like joy. I broke down the week-end he bought himself a tape cassette player.

'You never buy me anything,' I sobbed. 'And I can't buy myself anything because you eat all the housekeeping.' As I am a perfume freak and spend a fortune on clothes, this was neither true nor reasonable, but Hell hath no fury like a woman who doesn't get presents now she's married. Stricken, the brute rushed me out to the car and drove up to Victoria without a thought for his seat covers. At first I hoped he was going to take me to the pictures and a meal, but he bundled me into an anonymous little store and gestured round at dark shelves and a short, bespectacled proprietor.

'Choose,' he said expansively.

'What?' I gaped. Could this be a porn shop, in *my* condition?

'Choose yourself a cassette and I'll let you play it on my machine.'

After I'd run out of patience and new knickers and had flounced off to a different (male) doctor, who gave me healing things to tuck up my purple insides and cured me within a week, we realised that our marriage was going to be exactly like everybody else's. I am not without my little faults, like the way I spit when I lose my temper, throw things with deadly accuracy when I have a human target, and have total recall for multi-lingual obscenity which flows most freely when some vitally important business contact or strait-laced relative is standing outside the door with a finger frozen to the bell button and a petrified expression on his face. We used to observe this phenomenon, fascinated, through the spy hole into the hall. Sometimes the putative visitor rushed away before we could open the door.

My spouse retaliated by revealing himself as a sufferer from wind and athlete's foot, and spent hours conducting experiments with the tonic solfa and tins of messy talcum powder.

However, all and any of these little eccentricities might have been bearable if it hadn't been for the reading in bed. We both love reading in bed, but we read different types of book. I read the nails-chewed-to-the-quick, will-he-won't-he, sweat-on-the-forehead type thriller, while my husband likes funny books, the dirtier the better. He laughs out loud when he's amused and, because he's so hefty, his bed shakes noisily when he guffaws. People who've had us to stay cherish amazed and envious illusions about our sexuality and I've never liked to tell them it's the reading that makes the bed rattle.

Within a week of setting up home in Pimlico, I knew

I couldn't stand the roars of mirth that erupted every night at the precise moment when my chosen villain was sliding his stiletto between the hero's ribs. I just couldn't concentrate when my husband was lying beside me with hysterical tears coursing down his cheeks and epilepsy a sentence away. I begged him to read me out the funny bits in the hope that I'd be able to share the joke as well as its effects, but as soon as he cleared his throat and opened his mouth something went wrong. To my disappointment, I could never see what he found so funny, and I made the mistake of saying so. This led to countless rows of the restrained 'Go boil your head' variety and many weeks passed before I realised I'd married a natural-born Bowdler who euphemised everything and then locked up his bedside cabinet so I couldn't get at the originals.

Not surprisingly, other women's husbands began to resume their old pre-marital importance.

Men look so attractive when you don't have to wash their underpants, and I've always found other women's husbands money for old rope. They don't mutilate themselves with razors you've used on your legs, they don't have breakfast with you when you're hung over and someone is standing behind your eyeballs serving aces at the back of your skull, and they don't have to put up with being repulsed when you don't feel like it and attacked when you do. Sometimes they imagine wistfully that you might not be an ordinary woman at all, in contrast to their own dull wives. No wonder they're such a constant source of joy and free dinners.

For a while life picked up again, despite domestic discord, and I flirted with people at parties (I always have the same cycle at parties: chatty, randy, soppy, unconscious) and my husband flirted with other people at parties (but then he'd never stopped), when suddenly we began to notice that everybody was getting divorced, and the funny thing about the friends we knew who got divorced was that they started talking to one another for the first time in years. Some of them even began living together again. You'd meet an ex-wife with a gigantic shopping basket over one arm, grinning like an idiot and nattering about getting her ex-husband's dinner. For ages we couldn't get through to one woman on the 'phone and then found out she'd been helping her ex-husband move into his new flat.

'He never was any good at paper hanging,' she said happily. 'Used to drive me up the wall, if you see what I mean.'

It was all so romantic it was nauseating. I asked my husband whether we should get divorced for the sake of our marriage but he worked it out and said we couldn't afford it (being a Chartered Accountant he thinks about these things). I must say that was a very disappointing moment.

So there we were, with the number of married couples running out fast, and I had virtually no husbands to flirt

with and he had no bored wives to chat up. I'm tall and at social gatherings I used to find myself in a dark corner looking down on the disgusting dandruffy parting of someone on whom nobody would waste the legal fees of a divorce action, while my husband was stuck in another corner with the slag of the century, radiating corpse light. It was a very depressing situation for both of us, and I was struck by the thought 'My God, suppose he starts ringing up the best man again!'

I sat studying him one evening, when we'd been married a couple of months. He was sitting in an armchair with a drink by his right hand and an ash tray near his left hand. On his lap was a newspaper open at the closing prices, which was surmounted by an enormous heap of bills. For some reason he liked riffling through our bills. He never paid them, just riffled. His gaze was fixed to the television set as though he were homing in on it, and Disneytime was nearly over. Might this be the time to strike? I went into the bedroom and stripped off, which was brave for a start because we'd come to accept that the central heating in the flat consisted of mice running through the pipes panting. The cold did wonders for my nipples but ever since the honeymoon I'd known my husband was no sucker for mauve women, so I reluctantly put my clothes back on. It was at this juncture, as the police say, that I noticed a lump in my left breast.

I am no stoic; my pain threshold is so low I have to be given an anaesthetic for a manicure, but I was going to be very British about this development. Everyone would stand round my coffin saying how brave and calm I'd been.

So I went back to the living-room and shrieked hysterically 'I've got a lump in my breast', which had all the shock effect on my audience of a glass of herb tea. After a few more gentle verbal tugs at the umbilical cord joining my husband to the television the news began to seep through, but then it produced a reaction more outraged than sympathetic.

'You haven't been doing anything to yourself, have you?' demanded my spouse, peering at my bust as though he expected a report direct from the front. 'Everlastingly going on about how you wish the fat on your hips could be redistributed up top – now look what's happened!'

'Oh, yes,' I muttered. 'The wind's changed and I'm stuck this way.'

We were on our doctor's doorstep at eight the next morning, me wearing my Camille make-up and my husband full of cheery little comments like 'You'll still have your legs to fall back on' and 'You don't *have* to wear see-through blouses', which went ill with his bitten fingernails and chain smoking. The poor devil, a devout breast man, was, if anything, even more worried than I, and he glowered menacingly while our G.P. groped about amongst our communal assets.

'Not one but several lumps reveal themselves to the enquiring finger,' intoned the doctor, and I resolved that

I really should send him some more up-to-date magazines. 'Five or six each side, in fact.'

'My God! What's happening in there?' cried my husband. 'Billiards?'

Our doctor made soothing noises and an appointment with a specialist, and I went home picturing myself bosomless, with no one being able to tell whether I was coming or going, but when time had passed and my breasts had been fondled by several members of the medical fraternity it turned out that I had nothing more dramatic than chronic mastitis. Cysts, in other words.

'Cysts,' I carolled, dancing away from Westminster Hospital and barely overcoming the temptation to kiss a passing policeman.

'Cysts,' sighed my husband, closing his eyes to the price tags when I came home from my celebratory shopping expedition.

Cysts that wax and wane with the phases of the moon, part of my life now and impossible to overlook. It wasn't long before I began to wonder how I'd ever managed without them, although they could be a bit of a nuisance at times. For one thing, they weren't reliable.

'You're bigger one side than the other,' my husband would say, squinting at me as I dressed for a party, but the suspense riveted his interest, because we never knew what my bosom would get up to during the next few hours. I'd catch his eye across a crowded room and find that he was staring, hypnotised, at my chest, which had swung into its Sophia Loren imitation (both factions at once, thank goodness), and then with equal lack of warning I'd be able to sleep on my front four nights in a row because my lumps had done their Houdini bit. Equipped with unpredictable breasts that led a life of their own, I faced the world with new bravado and a fascinated husband. True, the cysts were sometimes so aggressive I felt as though I were carrying a couple of grenades around in my bra and had nightmares about exploding in the supermarket, but they were a lot more fun than silicone, and my Chartered Accountant could amuse himself dreaming up the lucrative routine I'd perform on the club circuit when we next fell on hard times – 'Alida and her Front, in Concert'.

Whatever the disadvantages of my undulating titties, they did wonders for our relationship and, blind to their faults, neither of us realised that we were faced with yet another symptom of my allergy to matrimony. I'd always been illness-prone, but after the wedding my case book started to make most medical encyclopedias look skimpy. in addition to my usual attacks of tonsillitis, 'flu and bronchitis, during the first six months I had thrush, mastitis, a duodenal ulcer, an irritable gall bladder and chronic constipation, and the way my luck was going I didn't dare sit down on lavatory seats. Along with my temper, I lost my anti-bodies when I got married.

Chapter Three

In contrast to me, my husband resolutely stayed the same; hungry and hirsuit. Age might eventually wither him, but he wasn't making any concessions to matrimony. Whereas the ailments I began to produce in alarming quantities all affected me intimately but were seldom discernible to the casual observer (unless he were a Peeping Tom with an exceptionally flexible periscope) my husband's afflictions rarely bothered him at all, but usually drove everyone else to the borders of insanity.

One particular matrimonial goodie I got lumbered with and could well have done without was my husband's ability to be mistaken for an Old English Sheep Dog which spent its days consulting the Stock Exchange Official List.

I was gazing moodily into the sink one morning when I realised that the time had come to explode another myth. That apocryphal Victorian Mama who instructed her daughter to close her eyes and think of England hadn't been referring to the marital relation (somehow I always think that phrase means my mother in law); her daughter had obviously made the same mistake I did : she'd decided to marry a hairy man.

As I tearfully scraped the thick, matted layers off my precious Madame Rochas soap, or dredged a couple of pounds of black angora out of the plug hole in the bath, I too thought of England. England, an island densely populated by hairy men, each of whom was followed closely by the stooping figure of a slit-eyed, maddened woman brandishing a vacuum cleaner. Were she mother, wife or lucky, she had my sympathy. I was a fellow-sufferer, wading knee-high through the overgrowth.

'What I can't understand,' I used to wail at my unmoved spouse, 'is where you get it all from. And you never seem to have any less! You're not even *trying* to get bald, just to spite me!'

'What I can't manufacture myself,' he replied smugly, 'I have woven for me in neat little squares, exactly the right size for bunging up sinks or making jackets for the soap. I keep a whole community of crofters in the Hebrides occupied from November to March and . . .'

But by then I'd usually thrown the goulash at him or slammed out of the flat so violently that the window panes were left lying in little splintered heaps along the sills. My temper wasn't helped, either, by constant reminders that I'd been told what I'd be letting myself in for.

'You can't say I kept it dark,' Hairy said, self-righteously.

The very first time I met my future mother-in-law she'd poured me tea with a shaking hand (twenty-five years of cleaning out baths with Sellotape) and said grimly 'Right from the start I think you should know that my son is very, very hairy.' There had issued forth a sigh so deep that two fairy cakes were blown to the floor. 'He's like his father,' she'd continued darkly. 'I thought you should be warned.'

I'd taken it as a joke, at the time. I mean, how melodramatic could you get? And about *hair*. After all the build-up I'd thought she was going to tell me he really did have syphilis, or was an impotent descendant of Jack the Ripper, and in view of her fascination for the area between the knees and the navel, what she had to tell me could have been so much worse. It's true that I didn't feel quite so confident about the triviality of the condition when I saw him stripped off for the first time. In a jovial, amorous mood, and minus my contact lenses, I'd thought he had some sort of furry combinations on, with erotic cut-outs for his working parts, like in *The Story of O*, and I'd asked him whether he wasn't a bit hot. He

hadn't taken my light-hearted comments at all well, however, and had delivered a lengthy and patently well-rehearsed treatise on the virility of the hirsuit male. To my horror, I'd realised that he was as nude then as he was ever going to get.

Yet still the awful enormity of the problem hadn't dawned on me. Point 1 – he has hair – had sunk in. Point 2 – his hair comes out – was as yet beyond my grasp.

'That's funny,' my mother said, squinting at a cushion one evening not long after I'd started going out with Hairy, 'the cat must be moulting again.' The cat wasn't, but it was combed within an inch of its life for the duration of the engagement. It used to go under the kitchen table and spit when it saw my fiance coming.

The hair had a direct effect on our sleeping arrangements. We spent months rowing in the bedding departments of furniture stores, while masculine assistants of both sexes sided with Hairy in pointing out the togetherness aspect of a double bed, and I retorted rudely that no inducement on earth would get me into a double bed with him. I knew that merely by resting my head on his pillow for two minutes I could magically transform myself from a blonde into a brunette, thus reversing the process it took hours of sweated labour in the hairdressers to achieve.

'Why don't you hand yourself over to Nair, in the interests of science,' I begged him, but pre-marital ardour didn't carry him that far. A vasectomy, possibly, but he wanted his hair left alone. Still, he did agree to single beds (except at the Savoy).

Now that we were married, arguments took on new dimensions. Newly wed and houseproud, I spent hours seeking out and removing hair from places I didn't even know my husband could reach. It appeared that not only was he in a continual state of moult, but what he moulted floated through the air, looking for likely places to alight. Paintwork was a favourite host, and I never dared to leave trifles out to set or put a first course on the table before guests arrived, in case the food acquired a new and decorative coating that hadn't been in the recipe.

'Oh, clever you,' a myopic redhead twittered one evening, when I brought a lemon soufflé through from the fridge. 'How do you get sugar to crystallize in these dinky little slivers?'

I trod heavily and meaningfully on Hairy's feet and grimly served him the whole top layer. He'd popped into the kitchen for ice cubes earlier on and left his trade mark on the soufflé at the same time.

After a little practice, I could track my husband through the flat with an accuracy that would have made Sherlock Holmes envious.

'You've been at the biscuits!' I'd cry, pouncing, during the agonising days when he was on a diet. Or: 'You're reading *The Perfumed Garden* again!' No physical evidence other than the disembodied tendrils of my beloved, I hasten to assure you. It's quite a good party trick, but I'm not the only one who can perform it. His secretary gets almost as much practice as I do, trailing his spore from the Xerox machine to the sales ledgers and from the dining-room to the lavatory.

Luckily it turned out that there are some minor advantages to having a hairy husband. Although the laundry lost three pairs of our sheets within a month, they never lost any that he'd slept in. Hairmarked rather than hallmarked, I suppose. And then, although he's quite attractive in a woolly sort of way, it would be a brave 'other woman' who got involved with him. One quick kiss and she'd turn into a brunette with five o'clock shadow. At least a wifely privilege is stepping straight under a shower when Hairy's been making his presence felt. I stand and watch the dark furry coating slip off and my own fair colouring return feeling all the nice feelings one usually has, and then I gaze sentimentally down at the plug hole and register the fact that the water stopped getting through some time ago.

My one hope is that bald people will start coming to him for transplants. The acreage is so enormous he'd be able to benefit a huge sector of mankind, and if the bald people also happened to be rich he'd never have to work again. There are other possibilities too. I keep dreaming of the day when film stars' chest wigs are made of my husband's hair, but unfortunately his fame hasn't spread far enough yet. Apart from his family, the only people who know about him are the laundry and anyone who happens to sit down in a chair he's just vacated. Chartered Accountants aren't allowed to advertise, so I'm going to have to rely on word of mouth, and in the meantime I can practise weaving his combings into rugs and knitting up blankets for the Red Cross. If ladies with dogs can do it, why not me?

Chapter Four

I don't know whether it's because he's so shaggy himself, but my husband does get on well with dogs. Wouldn't you know I'd be bound to prefer cats? I've had periods of acquaintanceship with many different animals, however, although living in a small flat precluded some of the more interesting ones. Not that my mother ever found a flat a handicap in that respect; during the war, when I was a baby, she even kept chickens on the roof, and we were living behind Jaegers in Regent Street at the time.

Eggs were hard to come by, but my mother was determined that just because there was a war on I shouldn't have to put up with that powdered muck. It looked like rather florid custard powder and might give an oriental cast to my features. Milk she provided herself for as long as possible and thereafter I honestly think she'd have kept a cow on the roof if she could have got one up the stairs, but for eggs you had to have hens. Quite how she obtained them I don't know, but although I can't remember it my mother tells me my early months were positively down-on-the-farm in pattern, with me cooing in my crib and a panic-stricken chicken bolting round our parapet, four storeys above Kingly Street, and laying eggs down the chimney. I'm sure what really guaranteed its yield was looking over the edge of the roof.

Not surprisingly, people in the street below used to look up, their heads tilted to one side in a listening attitude and expressions of disbelief on their faces. It wasn't every day you heard hens clucking away behind Hamley's, except during the time I was an infant, of course.

One of our poor benighted brood came to a sad and untimely end. My mother had good intentions but she didn't know how hens worked, and when her first protégeé stopped laying after faithfully producing an egg every morning for three weeks, she panicked. It never occurred to her that the chicken might need a rest, because she thought it was part of a hen's natural function to lay eggs. She was convinced the poor creature must be suffering from some peculiarly dreadful form of constipation and she had visions of the eggs piling up end on end until her feathery pet exploded with one awful, demented squawk.

Time went by and still no eggs, and the chicken, happy in its ignorance, blithely went on scratching around the skylight while I cried for my tea. My mother rushed off down the market and unburdened her fears to a butcher – not a wise choice, I would have thought, rather like going to a surgeon and hoping he'll cure you by Christian Science. Anyway, the butcher immediately said he knew all about chickens (amazing, considering he was born and brought up in Berwick Street) and that ours was suffering from a rare and fatal ailment which would attack humans if allowed to run on unchecked. My credulous mother went sadly home, captured the bird and took it back to the butcher to be killed. The best of it was she'd grown so fond of the hen she couldn't bear the thought of eating it and the resourceful butcher, who'd obviously banked on her tender feelings all along, happily disposed of the body.

My family's relationship with wild life also embraced rabbits. When I was small, Berwick Market had stalls with rabbits in hutches, and I used to push lettuce leaves through the wire mesh at the captives. The live lobsters outside the fishmonger's were nothing by comparison; I loved watching them move about but they weren't interested in anything I had to offer.

I had a maiden aunt who kept rabbits, and there would have been nothing remarkable about this if it weren't for the fact that she was also living in a flat in Soho. She certainly never thought there was anything odd about her household, and when I made it clear that I too was a rabbit lover, she promptly brought one round for me in a dangerously nibbled brown paper carrier bag. My mother remonstrated with her, so my aunt cited the chickens. My mother retorted that the chickens were productive, but unfortunately the rabbit was also proving to be productive, of little black currants all over the kitchen floor. Thus my aunt acquired yet another rabbit, and some of her collection grew so large and thumped their hind legs so enthusiastically we really thought they might be hares. Luckily the sort of neighbours you have in Soho don't tend to complain about the noise of hares thumping their hind legs on the floor.

My husband's idea of pets was very different from all this. He'd never lived in a flat, and to him an animal was a dog. When I met the people he knew, they also tended to regard dogs as the only proper pets, and for the sake of diplomacy for once in my life I shut up and listened to them yapping. I was glad I did, because what I learned about dogs made chickens and rabbits seem very tame. There was what to do when dogs were on heat, for example, and some of the tactics were highly ingenious. One lady used to gird her bitch into snug-fitting bright blue bathing trunks which looked rather incongruous on such a large white poodle, particularly as she had a curly and very active tail poking out of them like a dish mop. The catchphrase of the district was 'I see Mrs Oswald's Pansy has got her hot pants on again.'

Alarmed by the notoriety of the hot pants, a neighbour rechristened her own dog out of sheer self-defence. Her husband had called the animal 'Knickers' for the pure joy of watching his wife standing on the back doorstep and bawling the word into the gathering gloom of an evening.

'Not any more,' she said grimly. 'If we had a bitch in hot pants and a dog called Knickers in the same street the *News of the World* would never let us alone.'

It did seem that, contrary to report, the sex lives of

dogs left rabbits looking impotent. There was one long-haired dachshund bitch who'd fallen so hopelessly in love with her owner that when she was on heat she used to sit in the middle of the garden path waiting for him to come home at night and, as soon as he'd got out of his car, she'd turn her back on him, look provocatively over her shoulder, wriggle her hips sensuously and lift her tail up out of the way. Her master's wife said it was pathetic to see the poor bitch when the object of her craving gave her a brotherly pat and strode indoors. Whether this was his usual reaction to sexual advances I never found out.

Cats have more pride, more complex natures, better memories, and grudges. For years my mother kept a castrated tom who blamed the whole world for his condition. He hated men, probably because they reminded him of what he was missing, he didn't think much of women either, and the only reason he put up with us and a select few of our neighbours was because we fed him. It didn't take much to crack the thin veneer sophistication had formed over his dislike and I still have ragged scars on my arms which bear witness to his belief in savage corporal punishment, meted out for the slightest misdemeanour.

Our eunuch's sole concession to sociability was helping my mother to fill in her football pool coupon; it gave him a feeling of power. Sometimes knitting patterns would be used for this weekly enterprise and he didn't speak to us for days, but on other occasions numbers would be written on cards and spread out for him to paw and select. In the dim post-war years when people spent their free time doing things which didn't involve television sets, my mother's main hobby was writing to the papers, and one of the letters she wrote was about our cat's paw in the pools. There was a press photographer banging on the front door within twenty-four hours. He'd come steaming along from a national daily with all the photographic equipment he could carry and some very naïve ideas about the readiness of cats to participate in publicity stunts. It was mid-morning, the subject of all the fuss had gone out to inspect his boundaries, and my mother poured the impatient photographer innumerable cups of coffee while they waited for the eunuch to come back along the parapet. When he eventually did put in an appearance, the cat made it clear that whatever it was the newspaperman smelled of, he didn't like it. The photographs were taken under extreme duress and it is apparent from my mother's press cuttings that even retouching and careful guillotining of the prints couldn't wholly obliterate the claws or the claw marks or the savage expression of feline contempt for human folly.

Our tidied-up tom thought little enough of us, but when a neutered she-cat came to live next door but one I feared he'd have apoplexy. Up to then he'd had the freedom of the roofs and gutters (the chickens were fortunately

creatures of the past) and suddenly there was a militant, muscular female barring the way to the only house for miles that had a roof garden. (It's amazing how agricultural we were in Soho.) He shrieked at her for hours every Sunday morning (on other days he didn't bother to address her because the traffic noise drowned the choice insults) and finally there was a short, sharp exchange of blows and she knocked him over the coping.

He survived physically, but spiritually he was a broken cat, and he spent the evenings of his remaining years lying in his basket muttering about butch women. His only consolation was the television, when it came. He was too supercilious to watch it, but he used to squat on it, warming his behind, and his tail dangled down and made everyone look as though they were wearing a plait. You've no idea what it did for some of the polticians.

What with our eunuch and the chickens, and my aunt's rabbits, I saw a lot of animal life in London, but during the summer holidays I was treated to even more. My mother used to rent a chalet in Switzerland and we spent the summers there with another of my mother's sisters, who lived with us (sans rabbits). Perhaps the circumstances of my earliest years had affected me, but I was forever in the hen run chasing the chickens. I only wanted to feed them, but the hens didn't realise that, and being highly strung creatures to start with, they quickly went down with nervous traumas of various kinds and were usually in need of psychoanalysis by the end of the holidays. Obviously the way I squeezed into the hen house with them did nothing to help matters, but I thought it was sweet and cosy in there and I liked the snow-drifts of feathers. As I crawled in through the slit of a door, an appalled screeching would go up and the occupants of the wooden house would callously run each other over trying to get out. They must have thought I was an overgrown and exceptionally shifty fox, and the constant upheaval resulted in wild fluctuations in their egg-laying.

When I grew old enough to accept the sad fact that

they didn't like me as much as I liked them, and my pursuit didn't do their heart conditions any good, I used to content myself with walking down the sloping vegetable garden and throwing corn over the retaining wall, down into their run. Watching them scurry about pecking at the extra rations wasn't nearly as good as crawling into the hen house and trying to put the corn right in their beaks, but we all have to grow up some time.

Once a French girl friend of my mother's came to the mountains with us, and she was so absorbing I even abandoned the chickens and the goats to observe her. She was extremely emotional and drank quantities of brandy when the arrival of the post was imminent, but I could never understand why letters meant so much to her because every time she received one she'd either faint or scream. And that was before she'd opened the envelope! My mother explained that she was living with a man (my mother always explained things like that) who was a very uncommunicative type, so if he wrote at all it usually meant there was something badly wrong somewhere.

I was only five at the time, but I'll never forget waking up on the last morning of the holiday to find the French friend in yards of flesh-coloured crêpe de chine, rushing round the bedroom like a moth and sobbing 'My Bertie's run off with *Gingair*!' Since Bertie operated one stall in Berwick Market and Ginger (a heavy-handed lady with the henna) ran another, it was more like a merger than an affair, but the French friend was beside herself. Unfortunately she was beside us as well, and getting an hysterical emigrée and her luggage down a mountain and across Europe left permanent scars on my mother. For all the summers after that our only companions were the goats, the cows and the stolid Protestant couple who owned the chalet.

As a sort of retaliation, I think, my mother asked the French friend to visit our flat and feed and water the eunuch in our absence. It was a dreadful revenge to exact; our cat was a gourmet and expressed his dislike of

Gallic cuisine by picking up sheets of newspaper or even cushions in his mouth and carefully laying them over whatever dish his temporary cook had set down for him. If the food was fundamentally unsound, in addition to being badly cooked, he would not only hide his visitor's handiwork under the *Daily Mirror* or *Paris Soir* but would leap up on the kitchen dresser and hook some choice article of china into the air and on to the floor. Having reduced the French friend to complete prostration, he would then jump out through the nearest window and go to take tea with a furrier who lived farther along the block; the eunuch used the parapet like the Orient Express, before the defection of the restaurant car.

Missing the dreadful old martinet, I spent quiet hours in the Swiss attic, covered in friendlier cats, the camphor-scented Sunday clothes of the long dead swaying in the dusty draughts and brushing against my hair as I sat on the floor, reading the books left behind by generations of other visitors. My mother believed the only bad books were those that were badly written, so she censored nothing, and what with the goats and the calves and the memoirs of Casanova, by the time I was eight Bertie and Ginger had become completely explicable and very dull.

Back in London we were queueing up in the greengrocer's one day when the proprietress showed me a new family of kittens to which her cat had given birth, and typically I immediately wanted to know what sex they were. Rather taken aback, she said she didn't know. Her tone implied she didn't want to, either.

'Oh, that's all right, I'll tell you,' I said happily, and I turned the kittens upside down and ruthlessly passed judgement. I would have christened them as well, but we were in a hurry to get to the diary. I couldn't understand how it was that a grown-up knew less about such things than I did, but my mother suggested the question of gender might not play the part in greengrocery that it did in other occupations. Being a tailoress, she had a lot to do with men's clothes and this apparently gave her, and me, access to information denied to the less privileged.

I don't think it was the risk inherent in exposure to men's coats that made people say, all through my childhood, 'You won't put her in the trade, will you, Lucy?' as though it were prostitution instead of tailoring. Sohoites and practical to a fault, our neighbours' reservations were based not so much on the morality of any particular calling as on its rate of pay, and given this system of priorities they'd probably have ranked my husband's maligned profession pretty high, had they known more about it. Soon after I was married I knew more about it than I could cope with, and wondered in the dark watches of my sleepless nights whether Rasputin had really been a Chartered Accountant.

Chapter Five

It was more than mere habitual insomnia, or wild conjecture, that kept me awake all night after I got married. There were concrete reasons for my sleeplessness, like worry about insolvency. Rubbing salt into this open wound was my husband's overriding preoccupation with other people's money.

I've never regarded money as something to be hoarded or protected for its own sake but simply as a means to an end, the end usually arriving once a month in the form of a bleach job or a new coat or a visit to a gynaecologist, but my husband belongs to a group which regards lucre as a living entity, with a pulse and a heart and a temperature you can take at the Stock Exchange.

The first things I look at in a paper or a magazine are the horoscopes and the doctor's column, naturally enough, but my husband's first concerns are the closing prices and the exchange rates, and initially I thought the strain of being permanently overdrawn must have weakened his brain and he was calculating the growth of all the millions we didn't possess, under the impression he'd been adopted by Barbara Hutton.

Not so; whether he has any himself or not, a Chartered Accountant takes a serious and disinterested view of money. Whereas a typical greeting between friends might be 'I was sorry to hear about Auntie's leg,' my spouse and his colleagues rush up to one-another with commiserations about the guilder. It's not that they're warped, exactly, but they do take some getting used to.

We were sitting in the kitchen one morning and I was

miserably remembering how far we had to walk to the car through the pouring rain, when my husband came upon some scurrilous, flippant reference to his fraternity in a newspaper.

'The general public don't know anything about Chartered Accountants,' he said savagely. 'John Cleese in a bowler hat – that's how they think of us. If you prick us, do we not bleed?' And he turned his empty eggshell upside down and put his spoon through it, so the witches couldn't use it for a boat.

You can't really blame the public. I seem to remember that the late great satiric mob on telly even invented a dance called the Chartered Accountant, doubtless to be performed at Stonehenge round a flaming pyre of Tax Returns. The myth of a Dalek in a bowler hat has grown up, with the attendant erotic symbols of furled umbrella and closely-clasped briefcase.

'You're right,' I said. 'They don't know anything about you.' As the wife of one Chartered Accountant, and having been secretary to another, I am unusually well equipped to expose the true nature lurking behind the daunting façade of the A.C.A.

It isn't generally realised, for instance, that they can't add up. My boss used to take his electronic calculator under his desk with him to add up his petty cash slips (and even then he got them wrong) and my husband's idea of a total was any amount right to the nearest thousand. Booze bills for £13.75 were disbelieved, squinted at and finally left to mature until they reached a level he could comprehend. So much for my friends' pathetic confidence when I announced my engagement.

'Someone to fiddle our accounts,' they shrieked, and pelted us with dinner invitations. For the first six months of our marriage, our social life consisted of trailing from one appalling meal to another. A typical evening would be spent by lonely me lying curled up on some strange candlewick bedspread, clutching my duodenal ulcer and wondering why everyone we knew was in a financial cesspit, while my husband sat in a darkened room (the electricity was always cut off) and studied notes scribbled on scraps of lavatory paper and old cigarette packets.

One night I was in such agony that I thought I was dying and went crawling along a darkened hallway to a living-room door. My husband was getting to grips with an out of work musician who wanted to put a winter coat on his Tax Return.

'It was bloody freezing in Edinburgh!' shouted our host. 'If I hadn't gone on that tour I'd never've needed a coat anyway!'

My husband straightened his tie (which the musician had been wringing) and attempted to put the view the Indland Revenue might take. I crawled back along the hall and decided to die on my own.

After untold agonies, it finally penetrated to our dimmest acquaintances that my husband could do just about anything with a column of figures except the one thing most necessary, i.e. prove to those in authority that what was going out exceeded what was coming in before any tax had been deducted, but by then I was a heaving mass of Barium occasionally managing to wave a limp hand at my husband through the window of the Outpatients' Department and even he, with his leather inside and unerring nose for a free feed, was beginning to baulk at driving to the outer fastnesses for the sake of a plateful of water and monosodium glutamate and a look at the chequestubs of some derelict who'd bumped into us at a party three years before. Besides, his feet were playing him up.

No one seems to know about the trouble A.C.A.s have with their feet. I think it stems from all that pacing of the corridors of power. A demented Tax Inspector once told my boss that he must have cloven hooves inside his shoes, and maybe he was right, for it isn't unusual to enter an accountant's office and find him clutching his boot, his face distorted in a rictus of agony. My husband's feet are immensely strange, vaguely objects trouvés, and reminiscent of those first creatures that edged their way out of the sea and on to dry land. I soon got used to the way he'd disappear into the bedroom from time to time with a pair of pliers and the shears, to minister to his big toe, and emerge wreathed in smiles and ready to tackle a Balance Sheet with the best of them. One of his friends was admitted to the London Clinic and rumour had it that castors were fitted.

But lame or not, your genuine true-blue A.C.A. can get very excited when he talks about money. This probably explains the fantastic sex lives led by many a Chartered Accountant and Articled Clerk, but it is not without its disadvantages.

'Why did he have to be an accountant?' the mother of an Articled Clerk once mourned to me. 'Other teenage boys go into the bathroom with *Playboy*, but he locks himself in there for hours on end with *Accountancy Age*!'

The degree of excitement seems to relate to the sum involved, and days when my husband was due to discuss his company's fabulous budget were circled round in my diary like welcome home week-ends for sailors, because he'd come in like someone who'd just taken Crete. I remember one connubial evening when he asked me to phone the wife of a colleague.

'Whatever for?' I asked tetchily. I was comfortable where I was; the floor does wonders for my bad back.

'It was an interesting meeting,' he kept repeating. 'I think you ought to ring up and see how she is.' As said wife was a bit on the chilly side, a faint light began to dawn in my pea-sized brain and I tottered to the telephone.

'Me?' came a rather high-pitched voice from the other end of the line. 'I'm quite all right. Nothing wrong with me, I'm fine.' Her voice had gone up a whole octave by then. 'But John stopped the car and raped a pig on the way home.'

There were blubbering noises in the background and I put the receiver down. It transpired they'd been working out the company's finances for five years ahead. Just remember never to leave the auditors alone with anything more nubile than a ledger.

Although it never seems to deter the ladies, another thing about Chartered Accountants is their highly distinctive smell. Bank of England ink is a contributory factor, but basically it's cigars, and the higher up the salary scale they rise, the denser the smoke becomes and the more it tends to obscure the exotic aromas emanating from their uneasy feet. An A.C.A. at the top of the heap is only visible as a small black cloud emerging from chauffeur-driven limousines and entering vast mock-Gothic buildings for discussions on the possibilities of the moon as a tax-haven.

But above all, beyond all, behind the seventh veil and beneath the seventh seal, is the way they behave at home. Under their ill-fitting pinstriped suits and regimental ties,

their halo hats and incredible braces, they are creatures to be reckoned with.

My husband (who is fairly undemonstrative for an A.C.A.) used to prowl about at home in the nude and specialised in waiting until some elderly gentlewoman was passing our ground floor windows, where-upon he would throw open the curtains and bellow 'Hello, world!' I think it's a tribute to his physique that during all our time in Pimlico he was never arrested, and in fact the elderly ladies frequently waited patiently for him if he was otherwise occupied in the flat. Mind you, they only saw the good side of him (the outside), and they didn't have to put up with his feet and his wind. I put the latter characteristic down to the enormous business lunches devoured by my husband and his fellows, but they say it's natural aptitude, and recite the tale of an aged accountant who used to roam his tennis courts emitting sounds both strange and sad and greeting people with an angelic smile and the words 'It's bad to hold it in.' Most A.C.A.s seem to regard this as a Rule of Life.

After days spent considering flotations, femme sole assessments, P.E. ratios and internal auditing, the night-time vocabulary of an accountant dwindles to 'Glug-glug' (in need of drink), 'Hungy' (in need of food) and 'Hotty Botty' (in need of a warm bed). His work over, the intrepid A.C.A. takes his sleeping pills and passes out, leaving his wife to munch her tranquillisers and wonder why she turned down a tailor. Perhaps only a tailor's wife could tell her.

Chapter Six

After a nine month gestation period which brought us to the brink of divorce, and prompted possibly by the same motivation that drives a murderer back to the scene of his crime, or a lemming to the ocean, we decided to take a much belated 'proper' honeymoon in the country where we'd got engaged. Little things like cost had become a factor, so we couldn't travel in independent style to the isolated villages we preferred, but we decided to book on the package holiday which ended up nearest to our friends, many of whom had opted for premature and inebriated retirement in villas and flats scattered about the province of Alicante. Since we'd all suffered major and often farcical disasters there, it's hard to explain why we liked Spain so much, but our passion for the country was like recurrent bouts of malaria, and I was even ready to brave the toilet paper again.

Torn between pictures of hotels that were yet to be built and pictures of hotels that were already falling down, I stuck a pin in a brochure and narrowly missed going to Romania. Telephone calls to residents for recommendations found everybody out or asleep, and the travel agents praised every hole in the wall with startling impartiality, but come September we had our travel documents and were standing on a blotchy, troop-worn, pre-war tarmac looking suspiciously at an eggbox that was reputed to hold eighty people, provided they did their seat belts up tightly enough.

Inside the stifling 'plane my proximity to my neighbour practically gave my husband grounds for divorce, and when I gingerly sprayed myself with cooling cologne I had to apologise for decimating the delicate aroma of six rows of assorted after-shave.

'This is ridiculous,' I said to my husband. 'I'm getting out now, before it tries to take off.'

'How?' he panted.

As usual, he had a point. The route to the aisle was barred by two enormously fat ladies with the sort of thighs to put you off cigar smoking for life, and even if you got past them and their precarious tonnage of Duty Free comestibles, the assault course down the gangway would have turned a paratrooper's bowels to water. Uncontrolled feet and legs, belonging to passengers above the 4 ft. 6 in. regulation height for occupants of such aircraft, stuck out at lethal angles wherever a row of seats ended. Beneath and beside the feet were bags containing all those things which were either too heavy or too fragile for the hold, or which had been forgotten during earlier packing. Perched on top of the human members and assorted freight were handbags and cartons of cigarettes, babies and indispensable baby-accessories, such as grandmothers, and the occasional straw hat.

In sweltering silence we taxied to the end of the runway and waited while the plane heaved, struggled and cleared its chest. Then in uproarious confusion we taxied back to the airport buildings and waited again while jumbled flight schedules were sorted out, and several hours later we took off.

Shortly after we became airborne, a fledgeling stewardess made the elementary mistake of venturing out of the service area and was nearly drawn and quartered by the enraged mob; if she hadn't threatened to withhold refreshments until she was released a very nasty incident might have occurred.

We already hated everybody and were loathed in return, I had a sore throat and a headache which I was convinced would prove fatal, and the man in the next seat had finally decided that he was on holiday and since it was obvious he couldn't get farther away from me without smashing a porthole, he'd make as much use of our togetherness as possible. When we could unbuckle our seat belts I got out my cologne again and sprayed him in the eye with it.

At Alicante we were prised out of the plane and transferred to buses, where we sat, disconsolate and steaming, until our luggage and the obligatory courier arrived, and then for the next hour or so we were led in rousing British songs as we rolled through the stark, disturbing, bleached land which no one was noticing. All I wanted was to die somewhere cool and wet where no one spoke English. Stockton-on-Tees, perhaps?

The eventual hotel presented a frightening appearance. It clung to a crumbling cliff, and around its bottom typically Spanish signs like 'Wimpy and chips' and 'Twenty-four hour tea' crouched uninvitingly. Pallid people who had been gesturing at table-tennis came to watch us disembark. I thought that, like us, they must only just have arrived, but I learned later they were to depart the following day, their pallor being due to the fact that they never left the hotel. After all, it was Spain out there.

Inside the hotel, however, strenuous attempts had been made to disguise the disturbingly foreign nature of the environment.

'At least the electricity is Spanish,' I said, when the lights wouldn't work. The electrician was also indisputably native; he naïvely attempted to produce light by which to see to repair the fault, and we watched in fascination while he took the switches to pieces when they proved ineffectual.

Candlelight is only romantic when you're too old to need to see what you're doing, and it attracts insects. I for one was glad when dawn broke and we could get some coffee and go out looking for the beach.

Despite the contraceptives floating in the water and the smell of rank Ambre Solaire, I do like Spanish beaches;

there's always so much happening. Friendly Spaniards are getting stewed at the beach bars from ten o'clock onwards and if you're female, under eighty, and have any breasts at all, your ego can be so expanded it may never retract again.

'There's a nasty wind blowing up,' muttered my husband, shrugging into the huge, shapeless, mother-knitted object which is his holiday security blanket. 'You'd better put something on.'

'How times change,' I thought resignedly, recalling how he used to spend his time persuading me to take things off. The sun was bright, my eyes were dazzled by all those nice dark men who were taller than me (at least until they stood up) and I didn't want to put clothes on. Like many women, one of the main reasons I'm so fond of hot climates is that they give me the excuse to strip off in front of multitudes of strange men with whom it is unnecessary to become permanently involved. I don't see why I should feel guilty about this foible, particularly as my husband's version of the same trait involves buying bathing trunks with a shorter rise every year. Any summer now he's in danger of looking like Chad.

The wind blew and the men ogled and I preened, and by the end of the afternoon I had hot and cold shivers and an iron band around my head.

'You're feverish,' said the little girl who ran the bar.

'You're feverish,' said the chemist, handing me a boxful of anti-biotics.

'You're a bloody pain in the neck,' said my husband, reeling in at three a.m. from a Customs Officer's going-home party and collapsing on the bed, which gave a martyred squeal and disintegrated.

In the morning I couldn't breathe and my husband telephoned a friend who promised to send us the most beautiful doctor on the Costa Blanca. Apart from his looks, the doctor was also enormously popular because of the generosity with which he prescribed the Pill on anything but contraceptive grounds for fecund local ladies who didn't want to shock their confessors. Voluptuous nineteen year olds took the Pill to regulate their hormones, sway-hipped thirty to forty year olds took it for their migraines, and ladies who were older swore it cured their rheumatism. Unfortunately I wasn't in a state to appreciate my luck with the medical Mr Universe and I just flopped about under his manicured hands and was told I might have bronchial pneumonia.

'Within twenty-four hours of taking these tablets,' declaimed the doctor, flourishing a package, 'you will be able to get up.' If he'd had a cape to fling round him, his exit would have been perfect.

'I hope these aren't his usual brand,' sniffed my husband, 'not the way you get thrush!'

They weren't, but I did. I hadn't realised you could get thrush from taking tetracyclin. The second honeymoon followed the first honeymoon's pattern too closely for comfort, and my husband's Spanish having made no progress he was reduced to standing in the chemist's and miming 'My wife's vagina is itching because she's allergic to antibiotics.' I'm not sure exactly what happened but he came back in a terrible frame of mind.

Before the week was out he was also pantomiming 'My wife has coughed so much she's got piles,' and the dispenser had taken such a fancy to him she only gave him my treatments in minute quantities, making sure he'd return again and again to the *farmacia*, which became increasingly crowded as his fame spread. I must admit that unless you've seen my husband miming my ailments their full impact cannot have been borne in upon you, and for an Englishman he can be remarkably uninhibited when the occasion demands.

When I was a coughing wreck but mobile, we made pilgrimages into the hills to see our friends, whose troubles were less ephemeral than ours. One long-term expatriate had supervised the building of a dream villa near Calpe and whiled away the twilight of her days waiting for main drainage to reach her.

'If only my lavatory was connected up to something,' she'd say fretfully. 'I'm sure it's not doing the poor thing any good, being cut off like that. Supposing the porcelain rots, not being flushed through properly, and what does vitreous mean anyway?'

Nobody could answer her, and we used to sit on the patio drinking ourselves unconscious and discussing the vagaries of the cesspit, when we weren't talking about the carnivorous fish in the pond.

The demon fish were a local legend, held in dread by the villagers ever since a stray dog wandered into the garden one night during a *fiesta* and was later found dead in a compromising position, with one paw in the pool. What had been everyday, somewhat uninvolved goldfish gained the reputation of piranhas, and our friend couldn't get anything delivered for months because the local inhabitants refused to walk past the pond for fear they'd be dragged into it and torn to pieces. At least that was what they said when the unhappy owner of the killer fish and the isolated lavatory phoned up and screamed for her Butane gas and olive oil.

Between eating and drinking and coughing and edging away from the obtrusive cesspit, I managed to enquire how another resident had come by a bandaged leg and a walking stick.

'Not the fish again?' I asked anxiously, but it turned out that the injuries had been the result of a gallant attempt at preventing the village rapist (a mongrel hound some thirteen hands in height) from deflowering a visiting Pomeranian.

'And I don't think the Pomeranian really appreciated being rescued,' sighed our disillusioned friend, massaging his ankle, 'though the tourist with her was grateful.'

'I can't see how you stick it,' slurred my husband. 'It takes three months for someone to change a light bulb, you live on anchovies and Entero Vioform, and half your pensions go on bribing the police chief to tear up your parking tickets. You're all suffering from one endemic disease or another, and *she*,' (gesturing wildly in my direction) 'only has to step off the plane and they start sharpening the knives in the local mortuary.'

There was a defensive silence which was broken by the sound of a visiting garage owner falling slowly on to the floor, where he lay belching. I really shouldn't have told my husband about the Spanish bits of my past, I thought. He does tend to dwell so and it makes him prejudiced. He's never got over what he heard about the commercial traveller, or the time my mother suffered brain damage on the beach.

As if to confirm my suspicions, there was a muttered reference to 'Sixteen cards in one post, indeed!' He must have been remembering the distant Spanish summer when the English boy friend I went to visit was too ill to stomach my sympathy and too weak to get up and take me out. Every time I put flowers on his grave in Alicante I remember he went to Spain for the sake of his health. Anyway, as so often happens when I'm ostensibly alone, I had a great time and lost much weight through all the exercise of pushing oak wardrobes across my bedroom door in order to keep out the inexhaustible hotel staff and the commercial travellers from Madrid who occupied the other rooms on my floor. One of the reps used to pound on my door while I was eating breakfast and when I appeared wrapped in an insecure bath towel and lightly dusted with ensaimada crumbs, he'd shyly thrust his latest gift at me and bolt off on his rounds of the province.

Nonplussed and excited by my virtue (which owed much to my fear of being squashed, the Madrileno being approximately 6 ft. 5 in. in height and weighing at least 200 lb.), he deluged me with such a weight and diversity of largesse that by the end of the holiday my hotel room looked like the twelfth day of Christmas and, failing a pack mule, I chummed up with two inoffensive landscape gardeners and got them so drunk they didn't notice when I gave them my hand baggage to carry along with their own. Even so I'll never know how we got through the

Customs. By the time the tedious hours in transit had passed and we'd arrived at Cromwell Road Air Terminal, all that anis had worn off and as I settled back in my taxi amid dolls and cakes and wine and pottery, and watched the bewildered, simple faces dwindling into the dusk behind the cab, I couldn't help feeling enormously relieved that my unwitting porters hadn't known my name.

The commercial traveller wasn't quite so guileless, however, and obtained my address from the cross and frustrated hotel receptionist who'd spent his nights ringing me up and pouring hot and totally incomprehensible lust down my bedside phone until I muffled the receiver with a pillow. For the next few years I received up to thirty postcards a day, sent to me from every town in Spain by my roving correspondent, and the flood was only dammed when I finally wrote to him care of the Alicante hostelry with the information that I'd be getting married the following week.

Such traveller's tales do not endear Spanish men to my husband, and neither does he relish the huge premiums it's necessary to pay on the complex insurance I insist on taking out before seeking the sun, but I refuse to travel unprotected since the time I went to Majorca with my mother.

For the first day of that particular holiday I was prepared to be content with the hotel swimming pool, but my mother has an even greater bee in her bonnet about the sea and beaches than I have, and she didn't waste a moment in setting off on her own with a loaded beach bag and an O.S. bikini. About twenty minutes later I heard a commotion and raised my head from *Playboy* to see the figure of a plump, blood-soaked lady, supported by a group of yattering young men. It took a full minute for me to recognise my parent, who'd fallen heavily on to some razor sharp rocks and was already several pints of blood lighter than she had been.

I helped her to her room, and hours of anxious, fruitless telephoning passed before anyone arrived who was actually in the medical profession, although the lay medics who thronged the hotel prescribed everything from brandy to a tourniquet (the largest wound was in my mother's head). Late that afternoon, with our spirits as low as my mother's blood count, we were driven to an imposing clinic where the surgeon in charge had a terrifying row with the bumbling practitioner who'd brought us. I couldn't speak Spanish at that time and it was impossible to understand why the surgeon was screaming, or at whom, but later I found out that he was merely doing his nut about my mother's parlous condition and demanding to know why she hadn't been brought to him immediately.

To us he spoke in an acrostic mixture of European languages, the clearest word he uttered being 'insurance'. I got the message that if we hadn't any money and weren't insured either, my mother needn't bother looking at her next month's horoscope, so trying to appear more confident than I felt, I waved our impressive £1 policies and our passports, and watched while my mother was forced into a dentist's chair and the gash in her head opened wide with forceps. She shrieked, I screamed 'Anaesthetic! (hoping this was a universally-understood term), and I threw myself across her like Pocahantas on Captain Smith. For a while the surgery was like Harrods on the first day of the sales, but nuns were called for and an anaesthetist put his head round the door, and we all became very twentieth-century again. The surgeon ordered X-rays and told me he thought my mother had a fractured skull, and his colleagues made sympathetic noises and patted the bits of me most handy. Nobody patted my mother, but she was past caring. Her wound had to be explored and sewn up, and when she'd been trundled off to the operating theatre I settled down to wait on a hard bench in a dark, marble corridor. After several hours, a shrouded figure appeared and beckoned to me silently.

'Oh, God!' I thought, 'She's died on the table!' But when I tottered into the theatre I found an expansive group of masked men who wanted to show me their needlework before the bandages were put on and the patient despatched to a ward. Unfamiliar with this practice, I didn't know what they expected me to do at the sight of my mother's unconscious body, with its shaved head and network of stitches, but I nodded (I was trying to prevent my teeth chattering audibly) and that seemed to satisfy them.

By now I was desperate for advice, and preferably in a language I could understand. It was all very well to promise myself I'd enrol for Spanish classes the moment I got back to England, but what I wanted was some coherent help right away in Majorca. The only people I knew on the island were a phone-less ex-Soho couple who ran a boutique in Palma, and when I was offered a lift to my hotel by an apparently warmhearted medico I accepted gratefully and asked him if he'd mind driving via my friends' flat.

Having looked forward to pouring out my woes, it was

a terrible disappointment to find the house dark and empty, and I sat down on the lopsided stairs with an arid biro and some old envelopes and frantically concocted a note which I hoped might rouse them to action without actually giving them heart failure.

I was achingly tired and I knew I had to get back to the clinic as soon as possible, because in Spain the relatives are supposed to move in and look after the sick. The helpful doctor drove through Palma and out along the coast, leaving my stomach far behind, and I wondered whether my mother would survive, and how to deal with the bills. Although we were insured, the usual procedure was to settle the various accounts and then apply for reimbursement, and as we were in trouble during the time of the most stringent currency restrictions, I didn't know how to handle the situation. Neither of us operated a bank account (my mother had brought me up to believe that only cash was moral) and the insurance policies might not be as reliable as they looked. There was that unnerving bit about flying back the ashes or the body, for instance. Would they fly back the body if it was still alive? And how about the body's luggage and relations? Just as I was wondering gloomily whether my mother had regained consciousness yet, and if she ever would, I noticed that the doctor was driving with one hand and attempting to measure me for a diaphragm with the other, and I spent the rest of the journey beating him around the head, shouting for help to other motorists and trying to get the car door open. I've always been very good at hitting men over the head, and it was a marvellous way to release tension; by the time we reached the hotel I felt lots better, but the doctor looked pretty sick.

I collected some clothes, ate a couple of oranges and took a taxi to the clinic, where I found my mother alive again but noticeably dottier than before the accident, and we were settling down in our respective iron cots when a great hammering on the door preceded the entry of an energetic nun and our Palma friends, who'd found my note when they got home from a party and had come straight round to us. My mother's head was heavily bandaged and her dark, deep-set eyes and Roman nose looked even more dramatic than usual, but I still don't think it was very nice of them to say she looked like Valentino as the Sheik. They'd had far too much to drink to be capable of producing reliable advice, but their London accents and Sangria-sodden bonhomie were a tremendous comfort, and I sat up in bed to be kissed and petted, and to eat the food they'd brought. Perhaps there are substances that travel better than omelettes wrapped in greaseproof paper, but I was in no mood to be critical, and we talked and laughed and cried until three a.m., when the Mother Superior sent a minion to throw my friends out and we discovered that my parent had been asleep for hours.

The days passed and the fees mounted, and we only got out of Majorca because the nuns smiled angelically and took our thumb prints and photostats of all our documents, and the surgeon said we looked honest, particularly me. I'd learned that the less I wore, the more trustworthy the doctors found me, and I started modelling our friends' startlingly brief beachwear at the clinic. A disabled United Nations composed of ambulant invalids and their tired relations used to collect at the coffee bar on the first floor there, and while my mother was being examined I'd sit eating doughnuts with similarly occupied Swedish and German couples, dutifully remembering to tell them where they could buy what I had on.

Afterwards one of the meaner husbands went round to the boutique and demanded 25 per cent off the once-worn clothes, and a hot-blooded Swede bought everything at the first price asked and went away muttering 'Still warm' under his breath.

There have been times during go-slows when I could happily have eviscerated every employee of BEA, but I was so pleased to be going home on one of their flights, I was practically wagging my tail when I boarded the plane. My mother, wearing dark glasses and sticking plaster which didn't quite cover the bruises and the scar, looked exactly like a fleeing Mafia leader, and the other passengers avoided us to such an extent that we had the whole rear section of the aircraft to ourselves. We sat stretching our legs and giggling hysterically and made the steward so nervous he forgot to charge us for our drinks.

After our prolonged stay on Spanish soil, not being attacked took some getting used to, and my mother frequently came back from the doctor's very cast down by her sudden loss of allure, but at least we could communicate with our fellow men once more. It was depressing to discover how little we wanted to say.

Certainly I've never had a smooth passage in Spain, but it's all been highly interesting and instructive, and I'm sure the experience will come in useful some time. The thing is, my husband doesn't want it to come in useful. He hopes our lives won't require it. As I told him repeatedly when we had an eighteen hour flight delay coming home from that first married holiday and were marooned at Alicante airport with all the individuals we'd hated enough during a mere two hour hold-up, holidays are what you make them. He didn't hear me properly, though, which may have been just as well, because I was going down with congestion of the lungs at the time. Of course, I blamed it on the fog at Gatwick when we landed, but I don't think he was completely convinced.

I have the strangest feeling that it may be some years before I see Spain again; when I'm thirty-five, say, and nicely out of mourning. Did I forget to mention that the next visit would be over my husband's dead body? With all that's gone before, it would hardly constitute a change.

Chapter Seven

Despite his attempts to put his foot down, I never think of my husband as a boss. What with his hair and his appetite and his passion for crossword puzzles, he seems quite human to me, and in my experience that's the one thing bosses are not. Without going near a stick of greasepaint, any one of the employers who litter my past could make Lon Chaney or Boris Karloff look sweeter than Julie Andrews.

My first boss was a woman; I only knew this because men in drag usually achieve a better effect. After one week of returning jumpers she'd made the mistake of purchasing in a bad light, collecting quiche lorraine and smoked salmon from Fortnum's when she was having a dinner party, plucking her eyebrows and giving her face packs in my lunch hour, and locking up the shortbread at tea time because she was trying to lose ten pounds (only ten?) I was looking for another job. Not that I'd had the nerve to hand in my notice, you understand; I got the sack because I'd bought her the wrong shade of foundation when the shops were closing and it was too late to take the jar back and change it. Her complexion turned orange at a crucial moment that night and she never forgave me. Was it my fault she didn't have the presence of mind to say that always happened when she had an orgasm?

My next boss presented me with problems of a different kind. He was a fanatical long distance runner who sprinted to work from Stoke Newington every morning, giving more than one director an unwelcome jolt as he hared through the elegant St James's vestibule and into the lift. Repre-

sentations were made to him after the aged Deputy Chairman sustained a near coronary when my boss was late one day and put everything he'd got into a misjudged tape-breaking dash that fetched him up in the Executive Cloak Room with his running shorts round his ankles.

Although his sporting pursuits were not entirely trouble-free, my boss was able to take simple pleasure in many other aspects of his life. Me, for instance. He really enjoyed undressing me, and in those days it was a lengthier procedure. I should stress this was a strictly mental activity, but even so it was disconcerting, and rather than feel my garments melting off me under his thousand watt gaze I remained rooted to my desk hour after hour, longing to go to the lavatory, and typing on threadbare ribbons and transparent carbon paper rather than get up and walk to the stationery cupboard for fresh supplies while he was in the room. My predicament convulsed my unsympathetic colleagues, who continually asked me to 'Come over here and look at this' or 'Fetch me that file' for the malicious delight of watching what happened when I moved, but my boss had ways of making the others feel uncomfortable too, so they didn't go completely unscathed.

There was the way he smelled, for instance; everyone benefited from that. He used to get boiling hot running to work but it never seemed to occur to him to wash before he changed into a suit, and as a result the atmosphere in the office was like the inside of a furniture remover's boot. We had a whip round and bought him a stick of deodorant, and were amazed at the grace with which he accepted our gift, until we saw that he thought it was a cologne stick and dashed it across his forehead or applied it to his wrists to refresh himself while hunting up some fiendishly illusive payment. In those days junior staff were seldom seen and never heard, so we didn't dare to point out the real purpose of our present.

I was seventeen and, despite the weight of evidence to the contrary, I regarded everyone in the office where I worked as immensely sophisticated and knowledgeable – Olympian beings. I called all the men, including the lift-boy, 'Sir' and had palpitations if anybody noticed me. I was teetering on the lowest rung of the commercial ladder, a junior shorthand typist (now an extinct breed) and far above me on the snowy heights were the corseted ladies who were private secretaries to the directors. I never saw the dowager who acted as right arm to the Chairman; she communed with the world via a harassed little girl who was for ever running about the building with files or cheques, just like me. We used to bump into one-another with trays of tea in our arms. I seemed to spend the whole of my first year washing up and I was so nervous I broke seventeen cups in the first week and was very nearly sacked for the second time in my brief career.

Keeping me on to smoulder at and castigate when I used the word 'Blast' ('And where have you been spending your week-ends, Miss Baxter?') my boss the runner gradually revealed a few more of his ripe crop of idiosyncrasies. If he took his jacket off in the office, he considered it unseemly to reveal himself in braces, but his detestation of belts was so extreme that he preferred girding himself with knotted string to preserve decorum. For pleasure, he up-ended and searched litter bins, usually choosing the lunch hour to indulge himself in this habit, when the people in possession of the bins were safely out of the way. We'd often return at two o'clock to find him going over his latest haul, setting out on his desk top the booty which others had so perversely discarded. I remember he had a particular penchant for old pen tops, and string of course.

Then there were his economic wheezes. When new carpet was laid, he took note of the shortest routes between the various desks and the doors and proceeded to avoid these trails as diligently as if they'd been mined. Other people might wear tracks in valuable floor covering, but he wouldn't be a party to it. To see him swooping around the perimeter of the office, walking at least five times as far as was necessary to fetch the ledgers from the safe, one would have imagined he'd personally donated the heavy duty cord to the company.

'They'll be grateful for my forethought in the years to come,' he'd say proudly. 'Have you noticed, Miss Baxter, that by edging round behind those filing cabinets and past the window, you can utilise the door of the Invoicing Department when you want to go out into the corridor? A seldom-trodden stretch of carpet, that.'

My boss was in many respects a representative of a disappearing strain, but in those days his faith in the rectitude of the office hierarchy and his respect for the company's property were not as unusual as they would be today. With no provocation, the older members of the female staff were equally likely to itemise the unheard of blessings showered upon feckless modern-day employees, and a favourite pastime was hunting with bespectacled gimlet eyes for the faintest trace of dust left in the grim innards of a manual typewriter, or remarking loudly outside the Personnel Manager's office that it was one minute past nine and the red-haired hussy from Shipping was still in the cloakroom. They made me very glad I hadn't been eligible for clerical work in the 1930s.

I recall a particularly appalling scandal when one of the girls wore black stockings to the office, and all the senior secretaries rushed around and forced her to change into something decent in the lavatory, before a department head caught sight of her.

There was nothing greater to expect from life than elevation to the revered secretarial ranks, but in order to reach that distant goal you had to work your way up through an endless spiral of lesser jobs and menial tasks, and it was highly unlikely you'd get to the top before you were forty. If you married, you'd never get there at all. It was well known that the bosses didn't like their secretaries to be married; they felt the example of celibate priests or vestal virgins should be emulated, and decreed that nobody could be a secretary and a wife to the satisfaction of both the men in her life. Of the men in her life, her boss naturally had to be satisfied first. If you dared to get married, it was in secret, in a crypt, and you weren't fool enough to invite anyone who might be after your job because they'd rush off and tell on you.

This unnatural state of affairs led to a bitchy, hothouse atmosphere, where one had to walk a narrow line between being a despised wallflower with no boy friends and a potential hasbeen on the verge of engagement and inevitable dismissal.

For some reason, it was all right for the girls who worked the accounting machines to be married, and the stencil typists, canteen hands, tea ladies, comptometer operators and post girls were also allowed to mate, but not the secretaries. It was as though the bosses recognised mating as a primitive urge which the lower commercial orders could not suppress, but they expected their special handmaidens to be above that sort of thing and to sublimate their feelings by thumping typewriters and stroking files. Of course, there were bosses who had different ideas for ways of working off excess sexual steam, but they were usually careful to focus their attentions on girls employed farther afield than their own offices. A colleague's helpmeet might be fair game, but what would the world come to if a man's own typist started sobbing passionately into the dictaphone or complained because her boss forgot her birthday? Such excesses were to be avoided at all costs. These touch-me-not tactics could be frustrating if the boss happened to be attractive, but it was better to be unsatisfied than sacked.

As the years passed, this excellent precept slipped from my mind and when I started work for an attractive bachelor whizz-kid, I made the mistake of giving him a languorous look over my shorthand pad. Never have I seen a man so jarred. He spluttered that his private files were in a terrible mess and I could spend the afternoon sorting them out, and though he knew what they contained surely even he didn't foresee that I'd still be poring over them when the clanking of the cleaner's bucket tolled the knell of parting day.

The files were one great enormous mass of love letters, or letters about love, and after I put my contact lenses back in I couldn't help noticing the signatures: Brian, Basil, Humphrey, Desmond, to name but a few.

Beautifully warned off, I began my stint as secretary to this homosexual hotpants and I couldn't have had a more fascinating time if I'd tried (and believe me I did try). Quite apart from the stenography I was supposed to be doing, there were all the other little things to be fitted in, like working out seduction menus for instance.

'Now I don't want him to be too full, you see. Nothing that'll lay on his delicate little stomach and make him uncomfortable,' my boss would say, prowling around the distant reaches of his desk. 'One's got to think of these things. And he mustn't have too much to drink. He might fall asleep or giggle and either way he'd be useless.'

'How about smoked salmon and escallops,' I'd suggest conventionally, 'and champagne.'

'Ah, yes, champagne.' A mistiness would appear in my boss's eyes. 'I do so hope he's reached the age of discretion. Do you think he's got a sweet tooth?'

'It's hard to tell from the photograph,' I'd sigh, 'but if he's that young he'd probably fancy an ice cream sundae for dessert.'

'Not on your life! If there's one thing I won't stand it's some little dolly being sick on me.'

In addition to these romantic repasts, I was required to plan menus for my boss's dog and to listen over the telephone to the interminable outpourings of his housekeeper, whose fourteen-year-old sister was the mistress of a middle-aged psychiatrist. What with all this and fending off the Chairman's daughter, who had her blind eye on my employer, it was a relief to come home to clean, uncomplicated old Soho after my days in the office. I even enjoyed my voluntary work as secretary to the local P.C.C., through which I met a charming and incredibly randy member of the Vice Squad and a nervous priest who told fortunes with tarot cards. We three used to go out to dinner together and I was so stupified by the things they told me that I almost forgot to eat.

'I could take you to a club right now where not one of the strippers is more than eleven years old,' the priest would say, crumbling poppadoms earnestly. 'And all this mugging that's going on – the old badger game! It wouldn't be so bad if the girls let the man *get* something but they have some poor dope pounced on before he's so much as . . .'

'Really?' I'd choke. 'Don't you think this is a bit too hot for Madras?'

The Vice Squad man would tell us in detail the circumstances of his last few suicides, and how a friend of his had picked up a severed head from under a Tube train and asked it aggressively 'What's your name then?', and later we'd go on to one of the multitude of pubs in which he could drink after hours. It was all very companionable and restored my faith in heterosexuality, if not in the self-control of the Metropolitan Police.

Affairs at the office became yet more involved, so that I didn't know which passionate messages were to be passed on and which ignored, and then my boss had a nervous crisis and settled down with an understanding friend. I'd hardly had time to file the congratulatory letters referring to his 'happy nest' and wishing 'you two love birds all the luck in the world' when the Chairman's daughter attacked him at a sherry party and started telling everyone they were engaged.

'But have you *told* her?' I asked my boss. 'You can't let her go on thinking you're just too gentlemanly to be true.'

'I've tried telling her,' he whimpered, 'and so has everybody else, but she only gets a fanatical light in her eyes like Joan of Arc and swears she'll convert me to women. I don't know which is worse, the thought of her pounding around in scarlet knickers, converting me, or the way she keeps insisting she really likes gay society and doesn't mind if I have my own friends. It's all lies, she can't like gay society. I had a dinner party the other week and she nearly went mad when Richard kept holding my hand. The whole business is too much for me.'

It was too much for me too, and I looked for another job. This time I chose a family man, meek and moustached, whose office I shared and whose peptic ulcer I came to know like one of my own moles. Three years before I joined him, when a sparkling M.D. had to be given more spacious offices, my new lord and master had been moved into a partitioned-off shanty at the end of a draughty corridor, as a temporary measure. He was still there.

'When are we going to be moved?' I demanded, after

the icy blast whistling up my skirt had given me an agonising attack of cystitis.

'As soon as they can fit us in somewhere,' murmured my boss, trying to fade into the eau-de-nil paintwork. 'I'm sure they're doing their best.'

'And he's a director!' I screamed down the phone to my friends. 'Where do you suppose they've stashed the managers – in a window-cleaner's cradle hanging from the roof?'

At that juncture I didn't realise the telephones were assiduously tapped by the switchboard operators who, not unnaturally, took a remarkably long time to deal with calls. I should have been on my guard when one of them said 'Oh, just a minute, the M.D.'s telling his wife what to do with her Barclaycard!' but I never thought they'd bother to listen in to my conversations. Unfortunately they were in the pay of the Personnel Manager (they needed to be, on those salaries) who could have taught the C.I.A. a thing or two when it came to running an intelligence network, and I was summoned to the Personnel Department and interrogated. Wasn't I happy in my job? Didn't I like working for the company? Somehow it never seems to have occurred to any of the people for whom I've worked that if it weren't for sheer economic necessity I'd have avoided them like the plague. My idea of company loyalty is giving your friends alibis.

I could have been a lot happier, I told my questioners, if I hadn't been cramped into a draughty cardboard box that might have been persuaded to accommodate two brooms, provided the brooms were married, and I would like to leave. This declaration opened a war with the upper echelons which, for all I know, may still be raging. No matter what I did, they refused to take seriously my attempts at resigning, even when I had such a stiff neck from the ubiquitous air-streams that I had to walk about the passageways glowering over my shoulder to see where I was going. It was supposed that by handing in my notice I was seeking to pressure them into providing my boss with an office suite. They ignored me and treated him like a combination of Machiavelli and Svengali. He used to sit tearing the *Financial Times* into quarter inch strips and rocking backwards and forwards in his chair so that at one moment his forehead would be pressed against a filing cabinet and the next his pate would graze the partition. I didn't rock, I seethed.

'You've never been easy to get on with,' said my mother, matter-of-factly, 'but having you look at me sideways all the time is more than I can stand. For Heaven's sake get out of that place before you freeze solid, you're beginning to look like Medusa.'

In desperation I phoned in my resignation, pleading a sudden attack of claustrophobia which prevented me from entering my office.

The Personnel Manager's spy network was up to scratch.

'You're ringing from a call box,' he said slyly, 'How can you stand it in there, with your claustrophobia?'

'It's got windows,' I retorted, 'which makes it a hundred per cent better than my cubbyhole for a start. Also, there's marginally more elbow room in here, and it's warmer.'

It took three months, but I eventually got my cards.

This business of resigning has always been a great problem to me. Apart from my very first job, whenever I've wanted to move on the most incredible inducements and obstacles have been put in my way. I'm sure it's not because I'm anything very special, but somehow bosses seem to regard a secretary's resignation as a slur on their manhood no less shaming than finding their wife in bed with another man.

'Go? Leave *me*? (The great me?)' they gasp. 'Why?'

'You must be mad!' hangs in the air, mercifully unspoken.

It doesn't matter that only hours before they may have been hitting you over the head with a file, screaming that their coffee has gone cold, wanting to know why you let them forget their great aunt's birthday, blaming you because the cat's pregnant again (you forgot to have it spayed) and generally creating Hell on earth; you're expected to take that sort of thing in your stride. You aren't actually human, after all You don't have any feelings. You may be kidded that you'll get your reward for meekness in Heaven when you die, but everyone knows secretaries don't have souls, so a secretary's Heaven is a sweet and nonsensical fairytale, like a doggie's Paradise, or Santa Claus. If a girl works for a man she must take him for better or for worse, with ulcers and without, boorish or civil, bearable or not, and if she leaves him his family will tell him she's an ungrateful slut and he's better off without her.

I'll never forget trying to calm down the tearful lady relative of one of my more volatile employers. He'd bellowed at her and she'd left his room sobbing.

'Please don't let him upset you,' I urged. 'He's been in a frightful mood lately and everybody's suffered. My life hasn't been worth living, he practically kicks me round the office.'

'Yes!' snapped the frail Dior-clad female, buckling under the weight of her diamond pins and her lace hankie, 'but you're *paid* to put up with that sort of thing. It's your job.'

I'd never thought my salary included a percentage for vilification, but obviously it did.

Having worked as a secretary for twelve years and changed my job at regular intervals, I have nothing but contempt for those spy thrillers where the hero isn't allowed to quit the organisation because of what he knows, and walks in fear of bloody murder. If he really wants to find out what a sticky time's like, the agent should work as a secretary in an office for about a year and then try leaving.

The campaign usually starts with drinks, lunch and the proffering of cigarettes, and hots up through the hands on the table gambit and the unsubtle mention of more luncheon vouchers. This is followed by less and less obscure references to shorter hours and longer holidays and, finally, crushingly and unavoidably, money. Then more money and yet more money. If you're perspiring but adamant, this is when the tenor of the conversation changes and the rumbling threats start. Words like loyalty, duty, trustworthiness and mutual dependency crop up with increasing frequency, but from now on it's all downhill.

I've watched while a copy typist was threatened with legal action and reduced to hysteria when she tried to resign, and I've lost count of the number of times I've been asked how I could do this to them, 'this' being one month's notice – the stab in the back, the final disloyalty, the evidence that you weren't all you seemed.

'Of course, she never was very reliable,' a man once said to me. 'A bit unstable. You know, a fly-by-night. He was talking about my predecessor, who'd left him after thirteen years.

To a boss, the only acceptable leave-taking is death, but it had better be after retirement.

A colleague and I once decided that the only way we could evacuate our dead-end jobs would be to get pregnant, but even then we'd be expected to work up to the ninth month.

'I'm so sorry,' one of us would have gasped, 'but can I have the afternoon off? I'm about to give birth.'

'What are you talking about?' would have come the reply. 'Your contractions are only ten minutes apart!'

On consideration, pregnancy wasn't such a good idea.

Whatever changes may occur, labour saving devices be instituted or informal modes of address adopted, the one immutable object in an office will be the boss, and the one piece of equipment he'll cling to, no matter how many machines compete for his favour, will be a secretary. Making his tea and fetching his papers, she replaces the servants he now lacks. She has to listen when he speaks, she can be dominated, teased, insulted or dismissed. A gift of perfume brings tears of gratitude to her eyes and if a deal goes wrong she's there to restore the old amour-propre.

A secretary is the Western man's geisha and I don't see him giving her up in a hurry. Just how long women will go on putting up with the Mr Hyde ego their subservience brings out in the men who employ them, I don't know. Like prostitutes, they fulfil a ritual social and psychological function and they have to be paid accordingly, but Mother, is it worth it?

Chapter Eight

Our first anniversary was looming up and the rough edges of our relationship had certainly been smoothed off, but unfortunately raw flesh was all that was revealed underneath. I suppose you could say we agreed to disagree on practically everything, but it would be more truthful to admit that we just plain disagreed, and our respective in-laws were one very fruitful source of argument.

For instance, my husband could never get used to the way my mother and I fought. Having tried to step between us and fallen an instant victim to noise pollution, he'd go out on to the balcony and smoke, or morosely ride up and down in the lift, but if he returned within ten minutes there'd be a united front waiting for him, peace declared, and either my mother would be making coffee for me, or I'd be making tea for my mother.

That I could wind up to Force Five and back down again to a dead calm, all in the space of minutes, was incredible to my husband, the more so because he was so unused to it. He was brought up to believe that people who loved each other didn't have rows but went round giving each other little hugs and kisses all the time, that there was no dissension in a decent home, that children didn't argue with their parents and that if you ignored an unpleasant truth it went away; then he married me.

My earliest childhood memories are of my mother and her sisters and their cataclysmic rows. It was unfortunate that three women so totally dissimilar should be so closely linked, but a lesson in family loyalty that even in the midst of a screaming match all hostilities would cease and battalions reform to deal with any outside threat.

My surviving aunt was always timid and self-effacing (she is also as unalterable and constant as granite) and despite their grievances her sisters constantly rallied round to help her in her negotiations with the predatory outside world. My mother might have the grillpan raised high ready to deal a death blow when she would suddenly remember she'd promised to go and see the tailor for whom my meek aunt worked, and extort the holiday money to which she was entitled. Breaking off in mid-harangue, my mother would grab her coat and go flying down the stairs of our flat, cannoning into the office people who occupied the building below, and muttering what she had to say over and over again so that it would flow from her lips in a coherent and uncontradictable stream when she arrived at the workshop. When she got back the grillpan would be lying where she'd left it, but she would be too busy delivering a monologue on the iniquities of tailors to remember that particular row for a while at least (sometimes for as long as half an hour).

When I was in my teens there was one aunt less, and I picked up her hand and played it. The arguments assumed staggering proportions and were triggered off by things like hair-does and my friends and the fact that I liked going to church. My mother had and has a profound distrust of organised religion, she feels faint and ill in church and has heard too many brothel tales from the old girls in the neighbourhood to entertain a high opinion of priests.

'You're not going there again,' she'd cry, flattening out a Sunday paper and choking on the toast, 'with those awful people?'

When I reflect on the characters of the male members of the choir and that the mildest adventure I had was when one of them tried to rape me at twelve o'clock one summer Sunday lunch time immediately after the service,

I'm bound to acknowledge that mothers do know best, but this doesn't stop us rowing.

Ours was not a home where one treasured up a grievance and nurtured it in the depths of one's bosom; in our flat, the walls shook, the windows rattled, we all screamed (except my quiet aunt, who was deaf and could have read or dozed right through World War III, and was often required to do so) and strangely enough we got on together incredibly well. My friends were always saying how nice my mother was and how lucky I was to have such a good understanding with her, but our understanding was forged in the flames of a thousand raging fights, and when my husband first heard my mother and me shrieking at one-another and threatening murder, suicide and arson, he thought the end had come.

'What's happened?' he quavered. 'What's gone wrong?'

'She forgot to listen to the six o'clock news,' I said, dead-pan, stepping closer to my mother, who had also assumed a beady-eyed, 'ware strangers look. 'That's all. I told her to listen to the news and she forgot.'

'But I could hear you three floors down,' stuttered my husband. 'I thought, I thought somebody was going to kill somebody.'

'She nearly did,' said my mother fondly. 'Just like her grandmother when she used to go for us children with her bare hands. Coffee?'

My husband had come to collect me after work and he sank down in a chair and said he wanted a drink instead. I went into the kitchen for some ice and started giggling with my mother over a letter I'd had, and I could see my husband watching us with a frightened expression on his face, and his hands clenching the arms of his chair.

'You really shouldn't talk to your mother like that,' he said reprovingly, in the car on the way home.

'Like what?'

'You're terribly rude to her.'

'But I love her, we can be as rude to each other as we like.'

This logic may not have been acceptable to my husband in the early days, but it was a thought pattern with which he grew very familiar as time passed.

The tactful leaving unsaid that went on in his old home was as baffling to me as my noisy dramatics were to him, and I used to sit with my mouth hanging open while previously affirmed categorical statements were abruptly reversed or accredited elsewhere, outrageous fallacies were uttered unchecked, and no one made any comment beyond a smile and a nod. A lot of nodding went on in his house. When I told my parent, her mouth also hung open.

'Do you mean *he* never calls *his* mother a stupid old bitch?' she breathed, an expression of dawning comprehension forcing its way across her face.

'No,' I said hurriedly, in case she started getting belated ideas about how mothers should be addressed, 'and his parents never disagree on anything.'

This last was such a riveting piece of information that the whole block had it within half an hour and it was generally agreed that I'd married into a very funny family. Considering the peculiarities of families in general, this was quite an accolade. After all, everyone's got someone in the family they could well do without, whether it's Great Aunt Ivy who's stone deaf and thinks the postman is a member of Black September, Uncle Tim who believes the Queen is spreading unpleasant rumours about him, Cousin Jeremy who has personally ensured that there is not a virgin left within a four mile radius of St Mary's Hospital and riffles through his paternity orders like a deck of cards, or just embarrassing old Grandma who will take her teeth out when something gets stuck under her plate, even when you've got a bachelor millionaire coming to dinner. They can be a burden, but you do get used to them; they've been around a long time. The trouble really starts when you get married and suddenly find yourself with a whole new bunch, ready minted and champing at the social bit.

In the light of past experience, I'm an ardent campaigner for the pre-marital assessment of in-laws and subsequent optional disassociation from same. Friends you choose, relatives you're born with, but in-laws?

We all know you've got enough trouble with your own Cousin Bertha, who stands on the landing every Christmas Eve after her annual glass of sherry, shrieking that she's been assaulted, without the grandparents you've just acquired who make Enoch Powell sound like Ghandi and both of whom have halitosis to boot.

'With my body I thee worship,' avows your oven-ready husband, 'With all my worldly goods I thee endow.' Right, stop there, that's enough. Nothing about endowing you with a collection whose idea of Sunday lunch en famille is to sit round the table giving you a conducted tour of their piles. You get married because you love somebody, but that doesn't mean you want to embrace every gnarled and warty branch of their family tree.

It's particularly bad for a woman, because unless you fight like a wildcat you lose your own surname, and there you are, in with his mob, after it's taken you all your life to get acclimatised to your own. All of a sudden you're identified with High Tea and Pilchards and the Queen's Speech, when your lot were Bolognese and the Old Compton Street type of freshly ground coffee, and Communism. You're the one who's supposed to adapt, and if he's been brought up to regard Beans on Toast and that great British staple, Argentine Beef, as Haute Cuisine, Heaven help you when you dish up the Ratatouille. The lover who let you get away with everything but curlers in bed before you signed the register will develop overnight new appetites that only Boiled Beef and Carrots can satisfy.

But husbands, if you work hard enough, can prove in time to be fairly malleable. They will eat what you give them rather than starve, unless they're rich enough to eat out all the time, and if they are what are you doing in the kitchen anyway? Eventually they will concede an inch or two in many directions, although it's as well to keep copies of the T.V. magazines handy when planning a wheedling session. How many of us have been repulsed with 'Great God, woman, Match of the Day is on in five minutes!'

Time brings compromise, but such flexibility is not to be expected from those upon whom you work your sexual wiles either in vain or at your peril.

If you invite them to dinner and carefully give them what they'd give you, rumours spread that you are starving their boy and he'd be better off at a health farm. Give them the sort of food you like and gossip starts that you're raving mad, have foreign blood and can't serve up a decent plain meal. 'Coats everything in sauces!' is damnation indeed.

You could go to them instead, get indigestion and drive home with your husband in tight-lipped, windy silence, but whichever way you play it, you can't win. Not unless you're as imaginative as a girl friend of mine, that is. She's always on a diet when she visits her in-laws, living for a whole week-end on a tin of non-fat milk powder and a packet of slimming biscuits, and when they come to her she never tells them what the food is until they've eaten it. Until recently, her father in-law had no idea he liked raw fish.

To add to the other complications, every family has its own conventions, bêtes noire and skeleton(s) in the closet. It's tricky enough tripping through the circumlocutions of one lot, without having to learn a new set of rules to apply to another. How are you to know, until the blow falls, that you're saying the wrong thing? *That* wrong thing was perfectly all right up to now. But suddenly you stub your toe on a cornerstone of his family's hearth and very bewildering it is too. It's a black day when stiff-necked husband reveals that no one mentions elastic stockings any more, after what happened to Uncle Ken in the laundrette.

Of course, there are some people who positively adore their in-laws and can't wait to get them, but this seems to be a phenomenon most marked amongst those who have few or no relations of their own. Considering the miniscule size of my family, I imagine the only reason I don't conform to this rule is that what my lot lacked in quantity they made up for in eccentricity.

Jim, an orphaned friend who hadn't even a remote second cousin, married a stunning girl and entered her large family in a state of utter euphoria, completely undeterred by hints that his bride's parents were O.K. but she had the sort of nightmare Grandma who's always hysterically funny so long as she isn't yours. On their first week-end visit to the family home (they'd met and married abroad) Jim noticed a tense atmosphere but put it down to the usual new-son nerves. Abruptly, in the middle of tea, the Grandmother shot bolt upright in her chair, her neck craning like a giraffe. With an agility incredible in such an old woman, she flung herself over to the window, shrieked 'I knew it! It's that Rene Holland in a red hat!', threw open the casement and spat with hideous accuracy into the street. More than ready to see the good in any kin, Jim alienated his mother in-law for life when he remarked that they'd really have something to complain about if the old lady went out in the street and spat in.

Unfortunately his words proved prophetic, when he was sitting alone in the kitchen one day. Grandma loathed him on sight and not only told everyone she thought he looked like a convict, but also that there could have been only one reason for their little Laura to marry him, punctuating her bitter remarks by giving the bride hearty thumps across the stomach with her knitting bag. Laura said if she had been pregnant, a few days of Grandma's treatment would have taken care of it. Yet to this day Jim remains a devoted fan of Grandma, despite her having leaned over the windowsill and spat in his eye, and taken the oil-stove out of the backyard lavatory at a crucial moment, in hopes of freezing him to death.

As far as I can see, the worse thing about in-laws is the fact that they are. If you meet them casually or gradually

formed friendships with them, the pressure would be off, and you'd be far more likely to laugh at what Brother Ted does with his socks, instead of muttering 'Disgusting!' and sniffing pointedly whenever the poor chap enters the room. But you get them with the wedding ring, bang, all in one indigestible mass. They scare the pants off you, and they've welded to you for life.

If you're the nervous type, you can actually develop allergies to them: their soaps brings you out in a rash, their dogs bite you, their children are sick on you, and you think you'll never complain about your own family again. I often feel that the greatest inducement to living with someone rather than marrying them is the absence of in-laws on either side.

Perhaps we could all campaign for a trial relationship with our mate's family. If we knew what we were going to be in for before we married the figures for nuptials might go down, but so might the number of divorces. The only thing is, the families would probably be on their best behaviour during the pre-marital run, like engaged couples, so I suppose you'd really have to be clairvoyant to know what you were letting yourself in for, and as most of the clairvoyants I've met have been in a worse mess than I was, they too must have their blind spots.

Chapter Nine

Like those people who'd think Christianity so much more credible and British if it weren't for the miracles, my husband finds the successes of clairvoyants far more disconcerting than their failures. He doesn't expect anything from the occult, so when something happens he's goggle-eyed, whereas I spend so much of my time glued to the aspectarian like a cat at a mousehole I'm satisfied by nothing less than one hundred per cent accuracy.

An aged crone in a sleazy booth has only to tell him that his eyes give him trouble, he's married, he puts on weight easily, he's worried about money and he's trying to give up smoking, and my bespectacled, wedding-ringed, plump, lined, nicotine-stained husband puts away his packet of fruit gums and the dog-eared chequebook he's been fingering nervously and actually pays her 50p in cash.

From then on not only his fate but mine too is literally in her hands. If she tells him to beware of tall women I won't see him for days, a warning to be careful with his money (what money?) means an automatic reduction in the housekeeping, and my life won't be worth living if she comments sadly that he's misunderstood. He usually interprets this last as confirmation of what he's always suspected – he's not randy, just normal, and I'm not normal, just chilly – and the bedroom throbs with activity and masculine growls of 'I'm not getting my conjugals!' That's bad enough, but I don't think I could stand another week like the one we spent after some twit at a party told us she saw two children in my husband's palm and five in mine.

The trouble is, he's fundamentally serious and I'm not. I may be cynical, but I've been meddling with the business too long, and I like taking liberties with Fate.

'What a load of rubbish!' I'll snort, over the meagre, doom-filled paragraph allotted to my Zodiac sign in the paper I'm reading. 'Anything better in yours?' And I'll ransack every rag in the house 'til I find some ridiculously cheerful prediction that'll give me sufficient umph to get dressed. Whereas my husband can have his digestion ruined by reading that all Geminians are in a dangerous phase and should spend the week in a bomb shelter, I pretend bravely that I haven't noticed doleful horoscopes, and concentrate on the best bits of my last long-range forecast. This optimistic sorting of the wheat from the chaff is no more accurate than a blanket acceptance of the worst would be, but it's nice to travel hopefully.

I've been intrigued by every aspect of fortune telling for as long as I can remember (it's a common phenomenon amongst those who have no fortune) and even at the very beginning of my amateur activities, the most amazing aspect was never what I saw in the cards or the cups or the sweaty hands; it was what I saw in the people who so willingly consented to be practised on – they wanted to believe what I told them. Sometimes the odds were virtually insuperable, but they did try.

'Someone very important to you has the initial R' was the kind of pronouncement calculated to bring an entire family to a standstill. Hours of searching through old photographs, letters and diaries might produce the triumphal evidence that Mum's second cousin went out one evening with a fireman called Reginald, but if even a link as tenuous as this were absent, a chorus of 'We can't have met him yet' would be raised. Similarly, 'a windfall' happily covered anything from a first dividend on the Football Pools to the unexpected discovery of some Green Shield stamps lying forgotten in the bottom of a shopping bag. I found out that everyone was thrilled to be told they had an insatiably passionate nature, and I never met anyone willing to deny that they were too kind-hearted for their own good. The meanest man preened and acknowledged his generosity, the plainest, oldest and most confirmed spinster gracefully accepted the news that she could expect a marriage proposal within the year, and the more cruel and spiteful the listener, the more ready he or she was to agree that they'd been misunderstood all their lives.

While elementary psychology and a talent for farrago suffice for small timers such as myself, the skills employed by the professionals would be valuable to any detective agency and are far more difficult to wield than real E.S.P. could ever be. Imagine trying to deduce someone's past, present and future merely from their physical appearance and behaviour. It may be pathetically easy when Sherlock Holmes does it, but the strain takes its toll. Perhaps that's why so many fortune tellers I've met are in such bad shape.

In the same way that I hesitate to buy an infallible get rich quick scheme from a destitute beggar, I make mental reservations when I listen to the advice of temperamental, much-married mystics operating from tenement bed-sitters.

I was only sixteen when a gypsy I'd consulted asked *me* to tell *her* fortune, but there is a difference between innocence and stupidity.

'Why can't you tell your own fortune?' I asked.

'The crystal's a bit cloudy today,' she replied. 'And besides, it's unlucky.'

The crystal had been clear to the point of vacuity for my reading a few minutes before, but bad luck was something else. Still, I harboured the experience and it formed the basis of what can only be described as my jaundiced attitude to the profession. Years later, in a devillish mood, I actually scooped a palmist and made off with her clientele, but perhaps this action was a little extreme.

I'd heard complaints from friends about the garrulous

unreliability and extortionate charges of an Oxford Street harpy, and one afternoon when life was dull I went and sat in her waiting room. As I'd expected, it was packed – a further proof of my 'They *want* to believe it' conviction. Gentle enquiries elicited the information that each of the eight ladies present had been to the clairvoyant before, and were back again now because they couldn't understand why the future hadn't happened yet.

'She was so good!' they exclaimed. 'But her timing's a bit out.'

We sat and waited while noisy manifestations took place on the psychic side of the partition wall, and I wondered heretically whether someone was complaining about the fee. The ladies all looked hot and bored.

'I have a go at this sort of thing myself, you know,' I said chattily. 'For fun. For my friends.'

A large woman raised her eyebrows at the friend who was with her, and my nearest neighbour asked if I read 'Prediction'. The minutes dragged by and the manifestations went on out of sight. I spent the time dropping little gems about typical Taurean traits and what to do if your son had a via lascivia, and the ladies began murmuring and shifting about restlessly like thirsty cattle scenting water. Finally one of them couldn't stand it any longer.

'I'm fed up with waiting here,' she snapped. 'Suppose we all went and had a cup of coffee somewhere, would you tell our fortunes?' There was a pause while I tried to look surprised. 'We'd make it worth your while,' she added hurriedly.

There was a mooing agreement from all sides and I was borne in triumph to a Quality Inn, where the waiters were so fascinated by what we did that they gave us preferential treatment: good service. It was quite pleasant, telling those ladies nice things for them to look forward to, and I felt particularly happy because I kept thinking of the palmist opening her door and finding that the birds had flown before they could be plucked.

Not all clairvoyants are avaricious, of course. The least predatory one I ever met was an ex-prostitute who'd had the spiritual call and, feeling she wouldn't be able to settle down as a nun, had taken up fortune telling instead. Whether or not she wanted to expiate past transgressions I don't know, but she refused to charge anybody for a 'reading', saying her gift would be taken away from her if she capitalised on it. I often wondered whether some dreadful Nemesis had put a stop to her former career and left this strange notion in her head, but I didn't like to ask.

It was probably a rotten, sneaky thing to do, but whenever I went out with someone I used to have him vetted by my ex-pro friend, and during my engagement I visited her every other day to make sure there wasn't a facet of my future husband's character left unturned. Dolly was a psychometrist, which meant that when she held a bunch of keys or a lipstick or a letter, visions formed before her eyes and she could tell you all about the owner of the object or the writer of the missive, and the prevailing conditions. She said it was just like watching television, very entertaining, and often the pictures she described were so exciting that I wished I could tune in with her. There was no doubt that she was remarkably gifted, for she could even hold an envelope containing a Christmas card, and describe in detail the appearance and character of the person who'd sent it, but Dolly's one big drawback was her terrible tendency to digress. You might fly up to see her with a contract or a love letter or the woman next door's rent book, but there was no guarantee midnight wouldn't strike before Dolly got round to the point at issue. If the digressions hadn't been intriguing it might simply have required push to keep her on the right track, but when she started reminiscing about the old days I could never bring myself to remind her what she was clutching, and why.

Although she occasionally adopted a repentant expression and downcast eyes, it was clear that Dolly had liked her work, and was jealous of her professional reputation. There was a great deal of rivalry between the retired ladies in Soho, although some of them hadn't practised for years, and Dolly, with less self-criticism than a Jewish friend of my mother who describes herself as an anti-Semitic Yid, had enormous contempt for scruffy war-time tarts. *Her* friends had been real pros, she'd explain with pride, and she herself had rented a fabulous flat in Bond Street, with a maid. The only disadvantage to the flat had been that it was at the very top of a house with no lift, and some of her more mature clients had suffered greatly in consequence.

'There was one old devil,' mused Dolly, entirely forgetting my husband's cigarette case, which she'd tucked into her bosom, 'who must've been nearly eighty, and he had asthma. I could hear him panting all the way up the stairs, every week. It was agony.'

'Agony?' I asked.

'Well, I never knew whether he'd make it or not, you see, and he was such a good payer. My girl and I used to stand in the flat doorway hanging on to one-another. Talk about nerves! The suspense was awful. I was always terrified he'd peg out on the stairs.'

'But if the stairs did that to him,' I gaped. 'What about . . . ?'

'Oh, *that*!' scoffed Dolly, fishing out the glowing cigarette case and preparing to do business. 'I took care of all *that*. It was the stairs he had to worry about.'

What with Dolly's stories of working holidays in Italy, naughty clergymen, and the time she couldn't get rid of a Wren, the psychometry tended to take a back seat, but what did come through was all good stuff. Sometimes it was too good, in fact, because I was often given incidental information about my friends, and it's difficult to face people when you know more about them than you should. How do you smile politely over dinner when you've been told your host will come down with gastro-enteritis next month, his wife is unwittingly two weeks pregnant (not by him) and their house is going to become the subject of a compulsory purchase order?

Dolly was also marvellous at warnings. My mother would meet her in the market and come galloping back to the flat to find out whether I'd scalded myself yet, and I always had. The predictions were so unnervingly accurate that I cursed Dolly's iron morals time and again – she'd decided gambling might also result in the loss of her powers, and wouldn't give me a tip for anything, and the infallibility of her foresight, coupled with her stubborn refusal to capitalise on it, frustrated me so much that I couldn't bear to watch racing on T.V., and had to go out of the room while my mother checked her Pools coupon.

Now that I was married, Dolly's interest in me had waned a little. She'd revelled vicariously in the diversity of my single days, and used to abandon her housework or her knitting when something I'd left with her started transmitting psychic messages. Our doorbell would ring and there would be our flushed and exuberant ex-pro mystic, come to tell me that a red-headed man was going to ask me out and I should go because he was not only rich, generous and sweet-natured but destined to sustain a fatal thrombosis within the year.

She liked my husband but couldn't disguise her disappointment at my removal from the district ('The vibrations in Pimlico aren't wholesome') and when we'd been settled there for some time she gave me fresh qualms by hinting darkly that we'd move farther still before we were finished. Our flat had a new debit entry every time I woke up, but did Dolly mean we were headed for the suburbs, which I called elephants' graveyards, or the vast wastes to the East and South of London? Sometimes Dolly won't tell you what's in store in case precognition has a bad effect, and this was one of those times, so all I could do was to read the newspaper horoscopes again, and wrestle with their ghastly ambiguity.

Noticing the way I muttered to myself and stood staring morosely out of the dirty windows at the fog, my phlegmatic spouse was surprisingly sympathetic, fearing I might be going irrevocably off my trolley, or losing my libido, which would have been worse. He was unsettled in his job and sat composing letters and writing off to box numbers, his tongue earnestly tucked into one corner of his mouth, and his mind fixed on the possibility of taking accountancy to the uneducated natives of some exotic foreign clime.

Chapter Ten

The second winter of our discontent as a married couple resounded with familiar themes. The power cuts were brilliantly organised to coincide with meal times and I had my ninth dose of thrush as an unexpected Christmas present. The situation with my in-laws was so tense that my husband searched me for sharp objects before we went to visit them, and the only way for me to get through a day at the office was to sit imagining that I was firing a harpoon at my boss's stomach. I was taking three Tryptizol a day and two Mogadon at night, and I felt as though someone were standing inside my head pushing knives out through my eyes.

My husband went for so many interviews his office began to worry that he wouldn't have a tooth left in his head, and every night we sat discussing the relative merits of Thailand, South Africa, the Persian Gulf and Australia as places in which to live. Pimlico, we felt, was driving us mad. This was a more tolerable concept than that we were driving each other mad.

I thought no salaried job would be much better than or different from the one I had, so while my husband projected himself to a frazzle and practised confident smiles in the bathroom, I tried to think of some hobby I could take up which would provide me with an outlet for my battened-down ire and at the same time take my mind off the grey gloominess of our home. In winter, being on the ground floor and right by the embankment, it was virtually subterranean, and I haunted Soho to such an extent that people thought I'd moved back. My failure to do so wasn't for want of trying, but empty property there was either condemned or held vacant by hard-eyed speculators. I pestered Dolly for more hints about the future, but all I got was the repetition that we were going a long way, and she didn't know when. I was so fed up I began to wonder whether the long journey would be to the next world after a suicide pact.

As if to nail the lid right down, sex was presenting us with more problems than can be faced by two passionate hedgehogs. After all, hedgehogs don't concern themselves with birth control. I'd been on and off the Pill like a yo-yo for a year, because not all brands stirred up my thrush and when you're as used to taking tablets as I am, one more doesn't matter. However, no matter what brand I was on, as soon as I was given anti-biotics for one of my multitude of ailments, the combination acted like a sledgehammer on a nut and I started hopping around in the bathroom shrieking again, and I now had to face the fact that I must come off the Pill for good and all. Probably because of what they'd been through, my delicate parts reacted to contraceptive creams and aerosol sprays as though they were oven-cleaners, which meant I couldn't sport a diaphragm with any hope of effectiveness, and the F.P.A. got very wary when I asked about an I.U.D. Not unless you've had some children already, they said. I'd heard of shutting the stable door after the horse had bolted, but had never been invited to do it before.

My husband refused to be given a vasectomy for Christmas, so we were back to the old Wellington boot type of contraceptive, and very trying we found it, particularly as most doctors told me it was only marginally safer than Vatican roulette.

I was sitting in the living-room one evening, counting my sleeping pills to see whether there were still enough left to do myself in, when the awfulness of it all came over me in a huge wave. Thrush isn't something you can talk about round the dinner table with the Bank Manager, and G.P.s merely write another prescription for Nystatin and say

'Next please,' but I had to get the whole business off my chest somehow and I decided to write it down. The story of my kill-joy ailment came to about fifteen hundred words when it was finished and was such an arresting tale of woe that it seemed a shame to leave the manuscript lying in my bedside drawer with the empty bottles, so I sent it to a magazine.

The New Year came and my husband heard about the kind of job he'd always wanted. The snags were virtually non-existent, he said, and I'd learn to like Lower Saxony.

'Lower *where*?' I bleated.

'It's in Northern Germany,' cried friends with maps. 'He must be mad. Don't you know people die of exposure over there, *indoors*!'

From all the places in the world, my husband had chosen somewhere colder than England! But the job wouldn't be falling vacant for another six months, and he might change his mind; there were such things as Acts of God, and me. In January there was an encouraging letter from the magazine, who wanted to buy the article, and I'd had so much to get cross and fed-up about that I sat down and wrote those out of my system too, and the magazine bought them, somewhat defensively I thought. The angrier I got the better I wrote, and one week I was so incensed that the *Sunday Times* took the resulting article. Life wasn't any better but I was getting paid for it.

I used to stand in the street and wave up at my mother, isolated in her flat until such time as the power flowed back through the grid and set the lifts in motion once more, and wonder when the lights would go back on again in London.

One day I met an old friend outside the South Kensington Underground Station. He seemed to be carrying three oil lamps, but it was dusk and I couldn't be sure. I thought he looked very old indeed, for forty, and he appeared to be having trouble crossing the road, as he was being continually accosted by excited passers-by who hadn't noticed the electric flexes with which the lamps were festooned. He was in a near fainting condition, and I helped him into a nearby pub, where it seemed at one time that we might never have to pay for drinks again, until the flexes were spotted.

'I can't stand the strain any more,' said my friend brokenly. 'I've been all through the Yellow Pages and nobody will do it, so now I'm setting out on foot. There must be someone!' And he put his face in his glass.

I thought his raving was due to exhaustion. 'Do you feel it's wise, carrying those things about with you at this time of year?' I asked. 'Next time you might be mobbed before they noticed the flexes. You could be had up for carrying inflammatory material.'

'That's just the point,' snarled my friend, snatching back a lamp which was being surreptitiously prised away by a sweet little old lady in a woolly hat. 'They're not inflammatory any more. What I want is somebody who'll convert them back to oil, and I shan't rest 'til I find him.'

As the winter wore on and the power thinned out, new patterns of behaviour established themselves amongst the demented populace. A kleptomaniac I knew stopped lifting beer-mats and ashtrays and concentrated all his attention on wrenching the guttering candles out of the bottles in twilit restaurants, and some married friends came near to divorce because each blamed the other for having Great Aunt Hetty's chandelier converted to electricity.

My husband made the pilgrimage to his old home and after hours of trawling in the attic came up with his boyhood scouting gear and an object which, he assured me, would give out heat when required. Subsequent experiments proved that if I suspended a hot water bottle from the (sadly obsolete) centre light fitting in the living-room, it gave out more warmth than my husband's instrument of torture and was far less prone to frightening fits of St Vitus Dance. Nor did it falter and expire when the eggs were still at the dribbly-ibbly stage, for the simple reason that I refused to be trapped into cooking on a hot water bottle in the first place. Not using a modern rubber one, that is; I wouldn't have turned my nose up at the old stone hot water bottle languishing somewhere in my mother's basement store. This apocryphal treasure was spoken of in hushed tones throughout the neighbourhood, as people speak of suspected Gainsboroughs lying in derelict barns, for the possibilities of stone hot water bottles were apparently limitless, and ranged from their ability to keep stews hot so that they might be devoured beneath the bedclothes during the long winter nights, to their use as a terrifying method of defence when one was returning home through unlit streets.

My mother had some very surprising offers for it (the stone hot water bottle) but she decided to hang on for a bit to see how the market fluctuated. Having made a corner in old birthday cake candles the previous year, she was a practised hand at the game and hoped to realise enough for a continental holiday by the end of the strike.

I spent what spare moments I had collecting anything that would burn. My husband's accountancy magazines were the first to go, plus the details of the thousands of houses we hadn't had the money to buy, and then our bills. We kept tepid for nearly three hours on window envelopes alone.

If it hadn't been for the surcease my writing afforded, those months would have been bleak indeed, but everything comes to an end, even your tether, and with the approach and passing of St Valentine's Day and Lent (I always go mad in Lent – it affects some people that way) our flat occasionally entertained a shaft or two of watery light, the porters were to be seen outside their cubby holes, men at the office left off their vests, and my husband knew he'd finally got his job.

'But I don't think I want to go to Germany,' I moaned. 'Couldn't you be an accountant somewhere warm, like Spain?'

He gazed at me despairingly. 'I really think the thrush has gone to your brain,' he said. 'I could take out a huge insurance on you and then move to Madrid, but the Commercial Union might get suspicious. They've bailed you out too many times already.'

There didn't seem to be any satisfactory reply to that one, so I sulked over my typewriter and let my husband get on with his Lord Longford act. He was scanning some articles I'd unwisely left under the table, and I made a mental note to remember that he went grovelling under there after old cigarette stubs whenever he was trying to give up smoking. I don't like my family reading my work and I don't enjoy criticism, particularly the kind I get from my husband, which mainly consists of shredding up my precious scraps of paper and screaming 'You can't write that'.

'You can't write that!' he screamed.

'Why not?' I asked patiently.

'I have never been circumcised!'

'So you haven't,' I said mildly. 'I'm not sure which would be easier to put right, the article or you.'

From such small beginnings great rows grow. My critic even went so far as to eat my last two tranquillisers, although he had the decency to be shame-faced about it later, and I drank the last of the liqueur brandy, but I wasn't shame-faced about that at all.

'You're unbearable lately,' spat my husband into the fuming darkness, at three a.m. 'Why don't you get your bloody piles seen to?'

Chapter Eleven

Some people have claustrophobia, some people have xenophobia. Ever since I can remember I've had pile-phobia. I've always been terrified of getting haemorrhoids. During my childhood the scary old grannies and bloated, fecund ladies waiting to collect their offspring from school were always found pinning my mother to the playground wall with stories of their horrifying, ever encroaching piles, and the hideous bane grew in my imagination until films like 'Dark Victory' and phrases like 'Prognosis negative' came to mean only one thing – not cancer, not brain tumours – piles!

Over the years I survived a surprising number of ailments, which attacked virtually every organ I possessed, and in the dismal small hours when I wasn't speaking to the man in the next bed, I used to talk to myself, out loud, planning to bequeath my body to the medical profession.

'I shouldn't bother if I were you,' my husband often muttered callously, 'they've seen it all already.'

And they had, except for the one pristine and highly-regarded section which finally gave out on that wretched Spanish holiday. I know that practically everyone gets something on holiday – pregnant, deported, arrested, converted – but when I had bronchial trouble I'd coughed my lungs up and something else down.

'Don't worry,' a friend had said calmly. 'It happened to me and I thought I was changing my sex, but it's only piles.'

As far as I was concerned, this was like saying 'Whoops,

sorry, you're a eunuch now.' I had the bane and it, or rather they, were obviously there to stay.

I threatened suicide (but then I'm always threatening suicide) and moped about feeling like a combination of Quasimodo and Camille. It was a 'here today, gone tomorrow, here the day after again' condition; the wretched things were unpredictable and used to put in an appearance at the oddest and usually most inconvenient times. At the doctor's they'd go shy.

'Can't see a thing,' the medical men would say, rumaging around in the most amazing fashion. But back at home I'd walk across the kitchen and boing! there they were again. My husband got very bored.

'Can't you have 'em off?' he asked one day, when I hadn't eaten anything for forty-eight hours because I didn't want to have to go to the lavatory. But when I investigated the possibilities I heard such tales from the crypt that I determined to die locked in a fatal embrace with my haemorrhoids rather than yield them up and suffer what a frank theatre sister told me was the most painful post-operative condition she knew. It was a colleague who eventually put his foot down about all the limping, sniffling and wincing that was going on. I'd been to visit him in the London Clinic and was on intimate terms with his extracted gall-bladder, and we used to swop analgesics for our ulcers over the *Financial Times,* so there was no need for modest reticence about my troublesome behind. Leafing through his private files, my saviour found he knew a man who knew a man who had a brand new technique, and my bum and I were despatched for a consultation.

I always fall for doctors (probably because I meet so many of them) and I was putty in the hands of the specialist from the moment I found he had an electric blanket on his couch and kept his instruments on a warmer, a refinement I would recommend to any would-be seducer. Central heating and electric blankets have been responsible for the loss of more virginities than Casanova.

We had a long discussion about the unpleasantness of having icy metal objects thrust up or down one's inside and the analogy to milking a cow with cold hands, while he investigated as far as my breakfast. It seemed I was a suitable case for his treatment, and the method was explained. Instead of undergoing surgery, the patient was given a general anaesthetic, and the lower rectum and anal canal were then dilated in the operating theatre. This procedure was later followed up at home by the patient, with the aid of a dilator.

The prospect of ridding myself of my unattractive appendages sent thrills up and down my recently explored posterior and I made arrangements to be admitted to a nursing home as soon as possible. This didn't mean queue-jumping; the treatment was available under the N.H.S. and the waiting list anyone came up against was for the vital preliminary consultation with a surgeon. If the case was very urgent, whether the patient were private or N.H.S., he or she could find themselves in hospital within a week, for strangely enough the more advanced and painful the condition, the more dramatic the improvement that could be made. I was told that the technique was practised in many parts of the world and throughout the British Isles, yet the medical profession was so bashful about it that to most people the treatment of haemorrhoids still meant hack and stitch. I wanted to lose them in style (some day that'll be my epitaph) and after a good deal of wheedling and an outbreak of pathos my husband agreed to treat me to my good riddance on the overdraft.

It was as well for my peace of mind that nearly a year was to pass before another doctor entered my life and took me out to dinner, to discuss some medical articles to be written from the patient's point of view. We talked about the fabulous dilated bum method and I tucked in to my meal with the appetite I invariably develop when someone else is paying.

'Fascinating,' mused the doctor, studying his wine and rotating the glass delicately between his fingertips, 'absolutely fascinating. Did you know that while you're anaesthetised the surgeon puts his entire hand inside your rectum?'

It was rather a pity that I'd just taken a particularly large mouthful of veal, cheese sauce and mushrooms, but if you are going to do what I did in a public place it's a neat trick having a doctor by your elbow before you start.

Ignorance is bliss they say (and they're so right), and on the operation eve I tiptoed trustingly into the nun-run home. I expected cloistered quiet and downcast eyes and met the jolliest collection of ladies I'd ever seen. Perhaps bottoms are funny? Rotund sisters insisted I kiss my husband goodbye (as usual, I wasn't speaking to him), exclaimed over my nighties, ran me a bath, took away my sleeping pills and pain-killers and then allowed me twice as many of them as I normally take because I was nervous and my wretched lumbar region was playing up. I had the earliest night I'd had since I was five, slept like a log and woke to a sunny morning and a glorious pre-med – much better than being drunk and lots of fun when you roll on and off trolleys, particularly when you've been dressed in an erotic gown that stops short at your loins and does up with little bows down the back. I got randy, as I always do when I'm intoxicated, and had to be restrained from undoing the bows and kissing the anaestheist.

The only really uncomfortable thing about the operation was waking up with what felt like a cactus up my tail, but whatever it was was removed after an hour and then I alternately dozed and threw up for the rest of the day. I was told that most people clamoured for tea and sarnies within an hour, but I'm funny where dope's concerned (being so full of it already) and when my spouse rang up in the evening I frightened the life out of him by retching down the phone. An aged nun took the receiver, wiped it fastidiously and said 'She's slightly nauseated at the moment. Could you call back?'

With nightfall I suddenly felt better and discovered a

ravenous appetite and an urge to communicate with everyone I knew. I ate plates of bread and butter, drank pots of tea and read a lovely, gory thriller before my sleeping pills took effect, and the next day I looked like an advert for wheatgerm.

I was just wondering whether celibacy agreed with me when my reflections were interrupted by a bastion-like nun.

'Now you go and waggle your behind in a nice warm bath,' she said, 'and we'll introduce you to your dilator.'

I was very intrigued. Was this to be a he, a she, or an it? Thoughtfully, I went to have my waggle and trotted back to bed rosy, damp and innocent. I was greeted by two muscular sisters bearing an enormous glass dildo.

'Oh, no,' I gasped. 'You can't . . .'

'The first time's the worst!' they cried, and despite my muffled protest I was briskly deflowered and left disgruntled, astonished and sticky with lubricating jelly.

'Who runs this place?' I panted. 'Gay Lib?' But the nuns drew the curtains (somewhat belatedly, in view of the other interested, over-looking wards) and left me with my post-sodomite impressions.

My husband had a fit when I showed him my dilator. First he wanted to call the management and then he laughed so much he choked on the grapes he'd brought me.

'What I want to know,' he spluttered, 'is who models for them.' And apart from gurgles about 'You're never alone with dilator' and 'Every home should have one' I couldn't get another word out of him. A rollicking nun bore him off for home-made scones and he didn't come back that night, although I heard bawdy songs wafting up from the car park some time later and surmised the sisters had been treating him to some of their 100 per cent proof sherry.

I went and had a chat with the man in the next room but one, when I could bow-leg my way along the corridor.

'And to think I never sympathised with queers,' he mourned into his Bovril. 'Ah, me.'

'Ah, me too,' I muttered, but I was pronounced incredibly fit and discharged the next day.

And that's how I came to have a re-sprung bum, no more dingle-dangles and a positive affection for the loo once more. My dilator and I still maintain our relationship, but with decreasing frequency, and my husband doesn't sniff with quite such marked disapproval nowadays when I disappear into the bathroom with an outsize tube of K.Y. jelly and my solid glass lover.

Don't knock it if you haven't tried it.

Chapter Twelve

At Easter my husband was flown over to Germany to look at his prospective working conditions and came back ten pounds heavier than he went.

'They all cook like you,' he protested naïvely, when I made ugh noises at his avoirdupois. 'Only more so.'

I groaned. I could foresee the swift return of the four stone he'd lost since he'd known me and my nagging. It was as inevitable as the incoming tide, and I don't make a graceful Canute.

My husband's greed is legendary, and off-putting when you first dine with him. If he's served last he rests his chin on the edge of his unfortunate neighbour's plate, gazing soulfully at its contents like a dog in a pet food commercial, and if he's served first he digs in and eats the lot immediately, holding out his dish for seconds before the host has helped himself to sprouts.

The only way of operating so that the food bills could be met by the overdraft and we didn't have to have my husband's bed constantly re-inforced to bear his weight was by rationing his intake during the week and only letting him eat as much of my cooking as he wanted at week-ends. This was working very well in London, where my husband and his colleagues often skipped lunch to eat their profit forecasts, but what would happen in a country where the main meal of the day was taken at noon, in quantity, and far from the supervision of weight-conscious wives? I brooded deeply but could think of no new and effectively savage technique for keeping my husband's appetite in check.

'You worry too much about weight,' said my mother

comfortably. 'I'd have thought you would have grown out of all that nonsense when you started cooking properly.'

'It's all right for you,' I retorted bitterly. 'You wear corsets.'

'Good things, corsets,' commented my husband, as he stepped cautiously out on to the balcony with his drink. 'You squeeze in the middle and everything flows over the top like an ice cream cornet.' Even through the splattered glass of the balcony door, I could see the wistful look in his eyes, and realised I was in for an energetic cheering-up session when we got home.

What with the food and the shape of the women, my husband really should have been born in the Edwardian era; he'd have been so much happier. He's for ever gazing longingly at the wasp waists and bouncing bosoms to be seen in costume dramas on T.V., and asking me whether I fancy a cheese sandwich to keep my strength up (my lumps do deflate sometimes) – an offer to which my response is rarely warm. But to do him justice, I'm sure my husband doesn't really expect me to descend to sandwiches as a dietary supplement. I may be no show stopper in the bedroom, but in the kitchen I'm superb.

It wasn't actually my intention to hook men when I learned to cook, more an attempt at dusting down my self-respect, but they're all such gluttons that if you can perform adequately over the oven (what *am* I saying?), like me you'll find yourself with more male parasites than you can handle.

My belated expertise with the hot plate came as a surprise to everyone, not least myself, because at one time it looked as though I'd never be prised away from my well-thumbed copy of the Plumber's Journal and my spirit level. It was my mother who was the feminine one in the family, and she made constant and happily inaudible comments about my latent mumble mumble mumble as she thumped her home-made bread on its bottom like a heavy handed midwife and I obliviously repaired the fridge or tinkered with the radio. If I had to have hobbies, why couldn't they be more normal, she wanted to know, like painting, her own neglected aptitude.

My mother's artistic talent had been strangely fostered when she was a child, by lack of food. Her father, a great one for non-profit making enterprises, was already suffering from heart disease when he opened a restaurant in the West End – a gesture which was taken by his friends to be purely philanthropic in nature. He died in 1914, in the German hospital to which he had been taken in Zeppelin-confused London, leaving four children, a widow who knew about food and wine, and no money with which to buy either. To add to the problems, my seven-year-old mother and her sisters were taken to task for their German descent and thrown out of the French lycée in Soho which they attended, and the new school my grandmother found for them wasn't nearly as interesting, or as imaginative, as the old one. The lessons were boring and art classes simply consisted of a teacher pinning up a kipper or a slice of bacon on the blackboard and instructing the pupils to draw it, although in order to spark off some enthusiasm for the work it was understood that the child who produced the best painting or drawing should be awarded the pinned-up food. My mother could still remember what food had been like, and she went home week after week with something to augment the family's diet – her first efforts at bringing home the bacon. The facility encouraged by ravenous hunger continued to develop, and at thirteen she won a scholarship to art school. Her family were not impressed by her rapturous accounts of the succulent still lifes she might be given the opportunity to capture; they needed money badly, and she was apprenticed into the tailoring trade, which was as good a version of slave labour as any other. Occasionally I could make her stop sewing and draw me a picture, when I was a child.

In a household totally devoid of men (my mother was widowed shortly after my birth and my meek aunt came to live with us before I could talk or protest) *someone* had to know about electricity and plumbing. I used to point this out, with a spanner in my hand, but my mother remained uneasy.

'All right, but you don't have to *enjoy* it!' she'd shriek, as I climbed inside cisterns and juggled with ball-cocks.

There was no getting away from the fact that I was having a great time, ball-cocks and all. For one thing I loved electricity, probably because of my early exposure to it. My mother didn't understand the way it worked and when I was a baby she used to balance an electric fire on the narrow windowsill of our bathroom while she washed me, content in the belief that if my chubby infant hands reached up and tugged the fire into the water, it would simply go out. No fears that we'd both go out with it. It's less of a mystery to me that I survived a wartime toddler-hood spent in a chicken-run top floor flat within spitting distance of the B.B.C. ('Oh, dear,' my aunt used to say absent-mindedly, 'there go the windows again!') than that I managed to grow up before my mother electrocuted us all.

When I was about ten, I insisted that the bathroom should be heated with an oil stove, but my triumph was short lived. I got out of the bath in a hurry one day and backed into the oil stove, and after that my mother could score in every argument we had, no matter what the subject.

'Oil stoves!' she'd snort. 'Safer than electric fires! The fire never scarred you like that. Now you'll never be a Bluebell Girl!'

With crude animal instincts of self-preservation, I chose the neighbourhood handyman as a father figure and spent hours in his workshop beneath Carnaby Street, learning how to weld metal, where to dig a cesspit, how to poison people with wallpaper and which restaurants in the West End had cockroaches and a resident Sanitary Inspector. I emerged from this apprenticeship with qualifications that were sadly pre-Women's Lib. No one thought much of my ability to repair electric irons, catch rats or install a central heating system.

'Yes, but Lucy,' the little tailors used to say to my mother, 'can she sew buttonholes yet?'

My hopeful mother gave me little pieces of vicuna to practice stitches on, but I used them to lag pipes.

So the years passed. In an area already overflowing with eccentrics, I was regarded as more than slightly odd. If you haven't lived in Soho it's hard to appreciate the old fashioned family atmosphere. The population bulges with French, Italian, Greek, Chinese, Maltese and Jewish groups and the female inhabitants are expected to lead exceedingly feminine lives. I was born an unknown quantity – English and C. of E. – and my peculiar habits were usually put down to this rare classification. Heredity was also blamed, much to my parent's fury.

'Must you always be mending the television when John comes round?' she'd ask bitterly.

The idea of being lumbered with me for the rest of her life gave her the jitters, and my early behaviour didn't encourage seducers. Even after the accident with the oil stove, my mother had nourished dreams that I'd end up as a showgirl with feathers on my head and nothing on my fanny, snaking along catwalks at the Lido like the girl next door, and my pedestrian, unfeminine way of life was one long disappointment to her. I'd flunked out of the Italia Conti at the age of eight, couldn't sing a note, couldn't do the splits, and standing still in the nude was out of the question because I caught colds so easily I had to dress like a cricket umpire. Strong men died of exhaustion before they got down to my underwear. If I couldn't or wouldn't learn to cook either, the outlook was bleak.

In the end it was typical teenage egotism that turned me domestic. I loved inviting friends home to dinner but got sick to death of their paeans in praise of my mother's cooking. She had been influenced by her environment, and guests entering the flat were bathed in the warm scents of enormous pizzas or assaulted with vast platters of Zwetschenkuchen.

'Here, taste this,' she'd cry, and I'd lose yet another boy to her crowded kitchen, where whoever he was would stuff himself with Konigsburger Klopse or ludicrously rich cheese cake fresh from the oven.

'We were supposed to be going out an hour ago,' I'd grumble, as my mother waxed lyrical about the new blend from the Algerian Coffee Stores, or explained what she did with bruised avocados.

'Oh, no!' the latest Ulysses would whimper. 'I haven't had my afters yet.'

At last came the day when a Queen's Scout I would have given my eye teeth for told me to trot along on my own because he wanted another helping of apple pie, and deadly battle was joined between my proclivities and my self-esteem. Winkling my way into the kitchen was like getting another olive into a full jar, especially as my mother thought my intentions weren't honourable and feared for her equipment, but I managed. I locked myself in with half of Berwick Market's produce and the flat's most prized French cookery book, and my parent went to Regent's Park and walked round the Rose Garden for hours in a state of acute anxiety, like a man outside a maternity ward.

I can't say I became a cook overnight, but the years of smelling and tasting good food, and the ages of standing waiting while my mother discussed cuts of meat with the butcher as though the calf were on the danger list eventually paid off. By the time I graduated to that stage of improvisation where the lack of an ingredient or two is a challenge rather than a disaster, my mother was a nervous wreck, but I could cook and I did cook all the time. I became so popular people tried to move in with their cutlery, and that never happened when I spent my time investigating cisterns.

The man I married has hollow legs and regards his stomach as an insatiable God to be regularly placated with offerings, and he married me to please his stomach. The rest of him has constant complaints, but apart from the question of quantities the only culinary item we really disagree on is the criterion of a perfect boiled egg. He likes them hard and I like them soft, and when I'm ill the one thing I never dare ask for is an egg, because if I do I get an object resembling a grenade, and while I feebly try to get my spoon into the unyielding thing my husband stands proudly by remarking that it must be a long time since I've enjoyed a snack like that.

Marriage doesn't leave you much time for plumbing, of course, but I sublimated my old urges watching others rod through our lavatory or unbung our drains, and I still nurtured day-dreams of a nation-wide strike of sanitary engineers, when at long last my true worth might be recognised.

Would I get the opportunity to express my repressed personality abroad, I wondered, listening to the strange noises coming from the kitchen pipes, or would I have to go on with my secret dream life, rich in its plungers and ballcocks and quick-setting cement? I'd heard daunting stories about the efficiency of the German sewage system, so they probably wouldn't let me near it, and anyway, cooking over there wasn't a habit you could casually cast aside. It was practically a vocation.

As the scales screamed in protest and my husband rapidly and guiltily scrambled off them, I pondered what course my life would have taken if I'd ignored the cheap glamour of the cooker and stuck to electric circuits and drains. At least I'd never have gone short of work in our block, knowing what went on in the bathrooms all around us, but then would I have been there at all? My husband was too considerate of his insides to marry anyone who couldn't cook, and I'd certainly never have gone to Pimlico on my own initiative.

The chortling in the pipes reached a crescendo and then died away, leaving me glowering at the membrane-thin wall. You couldn't even contemplate in peace in our flat.

Chapter Thirteen

Having thin walls is when a neighbour tells you he's got cystitis and you say 'Yes, I know'.

For over fifteen months, my husband and I had lived in one cell of the largest block of flats in Europe. We only knew our neighbours' names because we got their wrongly-delivered mail, but I could have told you more about their personal habits than those of my best friends, and I hate to think what they could have told you about us.

The couple to our right only talked to each other after midnight, were addicted to T.V. sport and Wagner, played very vocal hide and seek and, judging by their rubbish, lived on Schweppes Tonic and potatoes. They had muttered rows (we all learned to mutter, eventually) about whether their bedroom window should be open or shut and practised Yoga over the week-ends (probably to combat the effect of two solid days next to us).

The girl on our left believed in quantity rather than quality, had nervous breakdowns in her bedroom, giggly conversations with girls in her kitchen and sexual intercourse with men in her living-room. Her bathroom was always full of people of both sexes relieving themselves, talking to each other and, thank God, frequently drowning whatever it was we were doing in our own bathroom at the time.

My most embarrassing moment occurred a week after we'd moved into the flat, when I was sitting on the loo spending a penny and someone six inches behind me, hidden by green tiles and the bathroom cabinet, started doing exactly the same thing. After a few agonised staccato bursts, the anonymous one and I both gathered up our drawers and fled. Over the months my bladder control became enviably discreet.

My husband's worst moment was lying in bed telling me a filthy joke and hearing the people next door laugh at the punch line before I did. He got into the habit of speaking so softly that everyone at his office thought he had laryngitis as well as bad teeth, and he used to come home rattling with throat pastilles donated by his secretary, who was obviously a soft touch.

It was as though every room was bugged, and we were reduced to secret agent tactics if we wanted to have a private conversation: we'd get under the shower, draw the curtains and splutter our confidences at one-another though the drizzle. Apart from anything else, it cost me a fortune in hair-dos.

When the implications of the porous walls sank in, entertaining became a nightmare. We'd spend entire evenings stopping our friends' mouths with alcohol, food and kisses, in the desperate hope they wouldn't end up blackmail victims as the result of some ill-considered comment, but we couldn't always be on our guard and the girl next door stomped past us in the corridor, eyes averted, for weeks after a friend of ours had been to dinner and given us a detailed account of what he did in Gay Lib, when he wasn't being a curate.

More humbling, we'd been made painfully aware of our sexual inadequacies, since we'd heard what went on six or seven times an evening on one side of us and three or four times a night on the other. I don't mind listening to other people doing it, but I don't want them to know when I am, and after I'd had to put a creaking board under my bed because of my bad back, we'd whiled away countless hours waiting 'til they all went out so that we could leap at one-another without fearing they'd pulled up their chairs for a bedside seat. But even this wearing ruse wasn't foolproof.

Languidly wiping away the perspiration one afternoon,

Sitting hunched in our living-room, with the Ride of the Valkyries thundering through from the flat on the right and almost drowning the keening of the girl in the flat to our left having yet another climax, I tried to understand why people wanted to live in communes, and failed. Surely you only had to move into a flat in central London and all society's silly, artificial little barriers were immediately stripped away. There was no such thing as insularity when you belched in an empty room and a disembodied voice said 'Pardon', but oh, how I wished there were. I knew I was just a neurotic hermit vainly searching for a cheap method of sound-proofing, but was I really alone? Wasn't there anybody else who wanted to go back to the days when you had to drill a hole in the wainscoting if you wanted to spy, or had modern builders brainwashed the population into accepting wall-to-wall eavesdropping? It might be a boon for the ear-plug manufacturers, but it was driving me nuts, and if I didn't have a break from it for a bit I'd go mad.

I put the idea of an early holiday to my husband, but he said going out for a walk would be cheaper.

Chapter Fourteen

It didn't do anything to cheer me up, knowing that my husband would only have to get me on Regent's Park Boating Lake to be within an ace of collecting the insurance money. I could tell when he was brooding on the advantages of my imminent departure; we went for a ritual trudge round Regent's Park every Sunday and if he was mad at me he headed for the lake as though it had suddenly turned to gin.

'Just half an hour,' he'd snap at me, a frustrated boatman married to a strictly non-amphibious woman. 'I like rowing.'

'Lovely,' I'd say. 'I'll cheer you on from the bank.'

'It's not as good on your own. All you'd have to do would be to relax and watch me work. It wouldn't kill you.'

But it would have, and by that time I was usually wearing my glazed expression (the one I'd collected as I signed the Register), if I wasn't pale green.

It's boats you see, and to a lesser degree trains, and cars, and buses and the Underground. As my husband says, you can't take me anywhere.

It all started when I was four, the first summer after the War ended. My mother packed everything, including me, my meek aunt and very nearly the eunuch as well, and headed towards the long-forbidden Continent. Unfortunately there was a little preliminary called crossing the Channel, and we had what was acknowledged to be an exceptionally rough trip. Everybody was ill, even the stewards. People lay in the companionways and half-in, half-out of the lavatories, helpless and pathetically convinced they held sole title to whatever bit of the ship they were prostrate in or on. It eventually ended, but I didn't.

'Alida!' declaimed my mother, in her yes, you are going to school voice. 'We have *docked* now.'

But I went on being sick. I was sick right across Europe, peering wanly out of dirty train windows at crowded, filthy stations, and recoiling from bowls of grey soup the French told us was coffee. I recovered when we arrived at the chalet in the mountains, but that whole wonderful first holiday was overshadowed by the dread of the journey back.

I didn't change as the years passed. I couldn't look at a toy boat in the bath without throwing up. I read *The Cruel Sea* with a basin on my lap. I walked a lot, because even bus rides turned me ashen and sweaty after a few minutes, and I learned to swim because if water ever barred my path, I knew self-propulsion was the only way I'd get across it.

The big breakthrough was planes. I loved them. From the moment I sat in one, dutifully chewing the gum they used to bring round in those days, I realised I was going to be all right. And I always have been. Scared, yes, sometimes (particularly when I had a boy friend whose speciality was flying through thunderstorms in the flimsiest of light aircraft) but not sick. And this is where we come to a gritty point as regards my marriage; another one.

My husband has spent Christmas Day crossing the Bay of Biscay, the only person to eat his way through the entire menu. He could ride a Big Dipper while eating roast pork and ice cream, and never feel a qualm. I call him Iron Guts when I'm not calling him anything worse, but . . .

The first time we went away together, I thought he seemed a bit strange on the day of departure. He's usually more placid than I am (let's face it – anybody's more placid than I am) but all that day he kept prowling about, ranting at me, and continually checking and re-

checking our luggage, our tickets, our passports, whether I was still me and not someone he'd never met before, probably a Communist infiltrator, whether I'd stolen his International Driving Licence for a joke, and whether I still really wanted to go. I did (not knowing what was in store for me). On the way out to Heathrow I noticed that he wasn't just sweating, he was *watering* everything anywhere near him. Perspiration was running off his fingers and splashing on the floor of the coach. When I tried to help him off with his jacket, it was like getting a diver out of a wet suit. And he was shaking all over. Really alarmed, I asked him whether he thought he had 'flu.

'No,' he said shortly. 'I don't like flying, that's all.'

To say he doesn't like flying is not merely an understatement. It was for people like him that seat belts were invented. If it weren't for being belted in, he'd try and leap out of the emergency escape hatch at least sixty times a flight. He doesn't speak to anybody, except to snarl, for twenty-four hours before a take-off, and I shall never forget the crisis we barely survived during our engagement when a strike left us stranded for thirty-six hours. If I hadn't been incarcerated in an airport hotel for the duration, I'd have got hold of some rat poison and put him out of his misery. I drank healing liquid and imagined what it was like to be dead, but he dripped and swore and smoked and steamed all the way from Dr Jekell to Mr Hyde and back again.

It's a shame that, like me, he has to have someone to 'blame it on'.

'How anybody who spends as much time as you do in the bathroom can claim an aversion to water, I don't know!' is one of his pet row-starters. If I was normal and seaworthy, we wouldn't be flying anywhere, you see.

As you can imagine, we have a problem. Either we travel by air, with him under sedation, or we travel by sea and land, with me on the danger list.

In our affluent pre-marital days, we did attempt a compromise involving a delicately timed meeting at Lisbon, but scant hours before I was due to wave my confident fiancé and his sagging car goodbye, there was a telephone call from an exhausted but thoughtful friend, who'd just driven down herself, through floods, earth slides, and roads that folded up after her, so we flew. Due to Iron Guts' pre-take off nerves, we had such a frightful row in the Departure Lounge that he wouldn't take his allocation of Duty Free perfume for me and I wouldn't take my allocation of Duty Free cigarettes for him, and that's the nadir as far as we're concerned. We sat as far apart as we could get and still be in the same plane, and I heard an anxious stewardess repeatedly asking him whether he needed oxygen.

It will be a long time before my memories of Portugal cease to be clouded by the aftermath of that flight. I didn't have the suitcase keys and was forced to join up in Lisbon Airport with what looked like a walking heap of kelp. The soigné gent I'd got my claws in over the pre-wrapped lunch stopped talking about his *quinta* and disappeared like an ice cube in a Turkish Bath, and the kelp collapsed on my lap, demanding alcohol and sympathy.

After we were married, we only agreed to fly to Alicante together because my A.C.A. recognised the indisputable economic advantages of the eggbox, and then he took care to be paralytic before getting the suitcases down off the wardrobe, but strangely enough he'd recently proved to be far better at travelling in aeroplanes when he was on his own. I suggested with less than tact that he might be growing out of his trouble, saying it augured well for his nail biting, but he swore it was my rotten company that turned his 'slight and understandable apprehension' into Grand Guignol.

'God knows how I put up with you when you're flat on the ground!' he grated, but I was determined to be optimistic. He'd flown to the Continent at Easter without horrendous incident, so I made preliminary noises about a Spring holiday and was dismayed to evoke the same old reaction.

'I'm not coming,' he said. 'Never again. Go without me.' To my astonishment, he meant it. There were all sorts of things he could do in London, he said mysteriously, and they didn't involve me or planes.

I stuck out my lower lip and vowed to go, plotting an article of yet more scabrous revelations about my spouse and his family by way of revenge. I wanted a holiday and I knew where, although I was now less certain on the travelling companion aspect. Girl friends I'd be bound to quarrel with (and I hated competition), any men foolish enough to be inveigled into a holiday with me would be inevitably and irretrievably scared off by my husband's awful warnings about my strange eating, drinking, sleeping and spending habits, and my only relations were my mother and my aunt. I didn't fancy a holiday on my own, because I wanted to have someone to grumble at, and it would also be useful to have a backstop around in case I misjudged the strength of those I flirted with. Such things had to be given due consideration. Already the thought of a husbandless holiday in a foreign clime was going to my knees, and my dreams became so erotic my husband started waking me up to complain about the language (I talk in my sleep).

I approached my mother, and she immediately sorted out the portfolio containing her will, her insurance policies and her Post Office book.

'Not Spain,' she said warily. 'I'm past it.' This was the cue for my master-stroke.

'I was thinking of Switzerland,' I mused, trying to maintain a facial expression which would convey innocence and lack of guile (my mother had been on too many holidays with me not to know what she was likely to be in for). 'If we stayed in Interlaken we could go and see the old chalet, and visit Berne, and . . .'

'Chocolate,' breathed my mother, sitting down suddenly. 'Fresh rolls and butter and black cherry jam. The Sessel Bahn. The walk to the Blue Glacier. The bald lady with the shoe shop.'

'Yes, yes,' I said. 'Well?'

'Well, of course,' she said. 'When?'

My husband drove us to Heathrow. His relief at not having to come any farther was touching to see, and that day he actually refrained from his usual quota of remarks about the way I'd earned the money for the trip (by selling vitriolic and uncommonly rude articles, mainly about him) or demanding commission again, or asking why the magazines didn't want *his* photograph. It was the most amicable scene in an airport we'd ever had and I was almost sorry to be leaving him behind.

The plane took off at a civilised hour and it was night when the coach that had met us at Basle rolled off the autobahn, roared around the lake and belted into the brightly lit main street of Interlaken.

It's a spindly little old lady of a town, reclining among ornamental gardens, cafes and shops, with its bonnet in the main station where the trains come in from the comparatively flat, gentle country to the North, and its button boots at the Ost, where the rolling stock of the Berner Oberland Bahn start out for the alps.

'I don't recognise a thing,' I muttered uneasily.

'Don't worry,' soothed my mother. 'You never saw it after dark.'

It was hard to remember what Interlaken had represented to me when I was a child. It had been the teeming town, an hour's journey on wooden slat seats from the thrombosis of Grindelwald, and the station there, the end of the line, had been a brisk hour's walk from the chalet we'd rented on the slopes of the Mettenberg. Sooner than climbing the mountain in the dark, we'd always arranged to get back before nightfall.

'Do you remember the tin bath in the wood shed?' I asked, as we inspected our quarters at the Edwardian palace of an hotel we'd decided to indulge in.

'Eight towels each!' marvelled my distracted parent. Then struck by nocturnal greed: 'What do you suppose the breakfasts are like?'

In a few hours, we found out. It was May, and when I opened the shutters blinding sunlight scorched across acres of carpet that could have been mown, if not scythed. A tray the size of a billard table was hefted in by a short waiter whose biceps strained at his jacket and whose expression shrieked imminent rupture. He grunted out, and we sat gaping over the expanse of silver coffee pots and milk jugs, font-sized porcelaine cups, towering heaps of rolls, ringlets of butter and dark oceans of jam. From the table on the balcony we could see that Interlaken hadn't changed, after all. The same horse-drawn buggies plied up and down, jolting tourists from one station to the other, the same shops dealing in carved ivory and hand-embroidered blouses lined the long walk between the meadows and the Kursaal, the same hotels sat on their haunches and ingested money, and the same multi-lingual exclamations of wonder at the views rebounded across the lake with the clicking of cameras. Three Japanese ladies in kimonos stood outside the hotel gates and photographed a Swiss farmer driving a calf to the butcher. They stared and twittered and the Swiss farmer stared stoically back and slapped his calf on the backside with a leafy branch.

'I can't stand the suspense,' I gulped. 'I've got to see Grindelwald straight away, before I wake up. We must have been in a time machine.'

My mother carefully buttered her third roll and glanced contemptuously at the corsets lying on the bed. 'Not just yet,' she said dreamily, 'after lunch.'

An assortment of nationalities packed into the little mountain train that afternoon. Tides of talk ebbed and flowed around us, but we sat in silence and stared at the long grasses sprouting from the banks overhanging the line, the miles of washing hung out beside the farmhouses and the new chalets jostling down towards the river. The pastures were pink and gold with flowers, and melting snow gushed over the rocks in foaming jets.

'Look at those beautiful cows,' said a reddened Australian, his mouth so close to the window that he made a little steam patch on it. 'Beautiful, beautiful cows. Look at their eyelashes!'

'Which d'you fancy, Cliff?' hooted one of his companions, from amongst the mass of haversacks at the end of the compartment.

'All of 'em,' sighed Cliff. 'I'm not partial.' The cows munched and drooled and looked at the train from under their eyelids. Even their dung smelled sexy.

At Grindelwald we climbed down on to the track and found the mountains leaning over us. The street still curved past the tennis courts and the chemists' shops still mounted judicious displays of purgatives and plasters, now thinned out with Ambre Solaire and After Sun. The dark old shoe shop was there, but the bald lady was taking it easy and wouldn't open until June, and then I knew I didn't want to see our chalet – there wasn't enough left of my armour coating and I couldn't have walked away from it ever again.

'If *that* turned out to be the same I'd go infantile and start climbing up the barn,' I grumbled.

'Not in those clothes, you wouldn't,' sniffed my mother, turning from a longing survey of the strawberries in racks by the grocer's scales. I was wearing brand new transparent white trousers and a top that had left a lot of change out of a very small remnant. Perhaps I wouldn't revert to childhood at that; I'd been one of the liberty bodice generation and I could still remember how they itched.

We took the chair lift to the second station, where there was a homely restaurant with a terrace perched on a crag, and sat drinking coffee and pointing out to one-another the places we recognised.

'The postman's house with the geraniums.'

'The restaurant where the cream's three inches thick.'

'The shoemender's chalet on the way to the glacier,'

'The little jeweller's by the bridge.'

I went for a walk, just to give the calories something to do apart from lying round my waist, and picked handfuls of gentians. The noise of the torrent from the crumbling snowfields was so overwhelming it drowned the rush and chatter of the chair lift and the humming of the wires between the pylons. I'd forgotten how beautiful it was here, and why I'd been so happy during those summers, and all of a sudden the dirt and racket of London seemed intolerable by comparison. Even my adored Soho was changing; half of Broadwick Street was scheduled for demolition, Ingestre Buildings had gone, and there were cranes and cement mixers and property developers everywhere you looked. Of the seventy-two flats in my mother's block, only half a dozen were occupied by people she'd grown up with in the area, and every time she went down the market somebody else had died. The muck had always been there, but things were different underneath.

As I stumbled back to the sunny wooden terrace and the smells of ham and coffee and potato salad, I admitted to myself that I was beaten and my husband had won the great 'leaving England' battle without firing a shot. Startled strollers would be able to hear my mandrake screams as far away as Notting Hill when I was uprooted, but it would have to happen and the fuss I made would be purely routine.

My mother was leaning back in the sunshine, a contented smile on her face and a little blob of cream on her chin.

'Why did we ever stop coming here?' she sighed.

Although we didn't know it at the time, the beginning of the end of our pastoral summers was signposted by the death of the man who owned the Mettenberg chalet. He'd been an alpine guide and as soft as a hawser, and when he loosed the reins his downtrodden wife started laughing to herself and bathing more often. She unplaited her hair and had telepathic messages from the virile young farmers around about (the laughter was particularly strident on those occasions), and considered it essential to collect cartons of noodles, which she stored under her bed until the massive structure rose up from the floor and hovered, very undignified, in mid-air. What the virile young farmers thought of the arrangement she never said. These innocent frolics culminated during our last holiday with her, a few years later, when we were roused to take part in midnight hunts for lost treasure and couldn't go for walks without meeting some fretful person or other who wanted to know what the widow was doing *now*. Her actions by then were governed by a strange box like a crystal set which emitted healing waves of radiation and thought-power, and life at the chalet was altogether so strange, particularly after I was kidnapped, that we never went back.

But that had all been in the future, the summer the alpinist died, and we were following our usual pursuits on the eve of the funeral. It was half past two and the chalet was quiet, except for the death watch beetle in the painting over my bed and the crackling of silver paper as my mother absent-mindedly unwrapped and devoured chocolate. I can still picture my aunt coming and rapping on the bedroom door, her Victorian nightie stiff with fright and her Colette-like hair even wilder than usual.

'I can hear noises in the end bedroom,' she said hoarsely.

My mother had been reading a book by George Adamski and choked on her Toblerone, momentarily shaken by the confused idea that Venusians might be responsible for the disturbance. I was deep in Berta Ruck and didn't look up, but I did register the fact that there shouldn't have been any noises in the end bedroom, which was spare. It was tacked on to the side of the chalet and you had to go out on to the large, eerie porch to find the door, braving the truly daunting stench of the earth closet which stood very nearby. It was a bedroom that was normally not used, but just at the moment it was occupied by the corpse of the landlady's husband, laid out in a coffin.

My mother and her sister held a conference, brewed tea and went to investigate. Before they disappeared completely, my mother popped back to ask whether I had my crucifix with me (I'd been going through an R.C. phase) but I hadn't.

'Never there when it's wanted,' she muttered, her lack of faith in the church patently reinforced, and pattered off into the unknown.

It turned out that the widow had thought her husband might be lonely and was sitting in the dark holding his hand and talking to him, but my meek aunt prowled through the house like a wraith for the rest of the night, and had terrible indigestion all next day from drinking too much tea.

'You know why we stopped coming,' I said.

Later that week we climbed the path to the old place, and there it was, but wasn't. The vegetable garden was a waving mass of dock leaves and stinging nettles, the hen run had vanished into rioting redcurrant bushes, there were only a handful left of the small white pebbles that had been brought up the mountain to make a terrace beneath the linden tree, and there was no wood. That was the most shocking thing of all, I think – the absence of chopped, split logs ranged up the walls of the barn for winter fuel. We looked at it until our eyes hurt and then walked back past the other scattered farms and sat on a bench to eat the packed lunch we'd brought. I was staggeringly hungry and gobbled at the crumbly rolls, thick with butter and filled with Emmental cheese and salami. My mother peeled the skin off some sausage and squinted in the pale clear light.

'I wonder what happened to the Beast,' she murmured.

Chapter Fifteen

The one really perverted way we'd occupied our time during those distant summer months was by feeding the local cats.

In rain and sun we carried bulging bags of lights from the butcher's shop in the village, and supplemented these basic rations with food we'd bought and were too tired to eat ourselves. If the wiry Swiss needed any confirmation of our eccentricity, this was it. Not only did we come all the way from England to a remote, inconvenient chalet for *fun*, and walk in the rain when we didn't need to, and bath every day in great discomfort and moral danger in a tin tub in the draughty wood store, we fed the cats. Obviously we and our landlady were examples of like calling to like.

The cats were lone creatures who fended and foraged for themselves, and when mice were scarce they caught grasshoppers and tore them limb from wingcase, crunching them up like pale green cornflakes. They drank spring water to quench their thirst and skittered off across the fields at the sound of human voices, expecting nothing good. But whatever early warning system exists in the cat world must have functioned superbly at high altitudes, because those independent, self-sufficient wild animals had us categorised and coming to heel within a week of our first arrival. A ginger cat came down the mountain and two black females came up from the valley, the smoky grey who belonged to the landlady presented us with her litter of four kittens and went off to start the cycle all over again, and a tabby from the next farm but one came and sat on our roof like the Statue of Liberty, in case any mendicants went astray and called at the wrong chalet in the dark. I used to gaze up at him and feel sure I could hear a Schweitzerdeutsch version of 'Give me your tired, your poor, your huddled masses yearning to breathe free' issuing from his parted jaws. One summer we were feeding thirteen cats regularly and had to cancel several excursions because we wouldn't have had enough lights money.

Cats came and cats went, but over the years the one unfailing visitor was something distantly related to a Persian, whom we christened the Beast, not because he had an unpleasant nature but because of his fantastic ability to transmogrify from a tattered, snarling wreck into a sleek, fat, stockbroker of a cat, once given the right quantities of milk and attention. Every summer we'd find him thin and scared, and feed him, every autumn he'd grow to look like Orson Welles and we'd badger the incredulous locals to give him food after we left, and then when we returned again the following year he'd crawl in through the kitchen door, an emaciated bag of matted hair and sharp bones, but alive.

One September when we were soon due to leave for home and had wearily abandoned the usual fruitless search for cat feeders, my exasperated mother wrote a letter full of bile and question marks to the London paper that had publicised the eunuch, and enclosed a photograph of the Beast at his most heroically pathetic. We went back to Soho, the cats climbed out of our feathers beds and went back to the fields, and there was an international incident.

Not only did everybody who'd ever said 'Ah!' at a carpet advert sit down and pour their feelings out on paper when they read the Beast's story in print, but the heads of animal welfare organisations throughout Europe, and countless incensed Swiss pet-lovers also took up pens and portables, and what they had to say wasn't friendly. Reeling under the impact of the mail bags, the Features Editor first tentatively suggested that his contributor might deal with *some* of the correspondence herself, then began wildly redirecting everything, and finally panicked and said some kind of retraction must be printed. By that time my mother was having to prime herself with brandy before facing the day's quota of criticism, condemnation and misguided advice, and she would have done anything to dam the flood. Our postman, who suffered from lumbago and muscle spasms, wasn't speaking to her any more. The Features Editor composed a short, neat letter to the effect that arrangements had been made with a trustworthy person who would feed the Beast and all the other cats in our absence, and this appeared above my parent's name in the paper. My mother drily asked me to light a candle for the soul of the perjurer next time I was passing a convenient altar.

'I suppose something had to be done,' she sighed. 'But when I think of those poor animals . . .'

Not one of the well-meaning ladies and gentlemen who'd written naïvely from large suburban houses where up to eleven cats could be accommodated at a low rent (on the understanding that they were smuggled over, of course, for they would have gone mad in quarantine), nor any of the representatives of authority who'd wanted to know why we hadn't gone to Geneva for help, had given a practical or practicable solution to the problem. The mountains and the mountain people didn't change, and neither did the situation; cats were fed by mad tourists and not by hard-working farmers. but as far as the great warm-hearted British public were concerned justice had been seen to be done, and the case was closed.

I lit a candle for the Features Editor and another for the Beast, but my faith must have been a bit shaky and my C. of E. inclinations on the wax, for the paper closed, the perjurer went into Public Relations, and next summer the Beast wouldn't come indoors to eat with us but snatched at meat laid out at ten yards' distance.

'He must have been at least seventeen,' I said, 'the last

time we saw him. Work it out – he was two or three when . . .'

'I don't want to work it out,' blurted my mother, finding herself about to wipe her eyes with a slice of salami. 'It's so depressing. Poor old devil.' There was a mournful sniff and a flailing about with paper handkerchiefs.

'We used to eat salads at that table under the linden tree, didn't we?' I went on callously, inspecting the contents of my next roll. 'With caterpillars falling on us? And I was always getting splinters in my thighs from the bench?'

'Yes, and the cats used to sit on our feet and eat all your Appenzeller for you because you didn't like it. They'd eat anything.' And she disappeared into her lunch bag. It was hopeless, really. Impossible to think of the chalet without the cats, stretching to be stroked, or the landlady, knitting as she talked and laughed to herself in her kitchen, or the old postman, cycling from farm to farm, criss-crossing the valley floor and reaching our path between three and four o'clock every afternoon. We offered him beer on hot days, and when I grew older and began sun-bathing the sound of his friendly voice and stumbling boots sent me leaping up and running to hide behind the barn. Funny, I was never more reluctant to reveal myself than in that brief, fresh out of childhood season before there was anything worth revealing. I was terribly sensitive about being looked at and went through hideous mortifications when the Swiss Army sent men into the mountains on manoeuvres. For weeks I was constantly obliged to clump past columns of the temporary soldiers doing their yearly fortnight's duty in drab, loose uniforms, suffering the way they stared into my burning face and made miaowing noises after me as I struggled with the milk cans or, clumsy with embarrassment, dropped and smashed the empty lemonade bottles I was returning to the kiosk by the river.

Even when they were out of sight the Army invaded my mind. They played strange roles in my imagination and their presence was a new element in my wholesome summer life. When they stepped out from under the pines and looked at me with such insulting intensity, they apparently saw beyond my straight hair and salt cellars and plaster-covered knees to the me I would be in a year or two, and I saw the reflection of the me ahead and was scared stiff. I became more childish as a perverse form of retaliation, and played tiger-stalking with the cats, kneeling up in the long grass by the currant bushes and clacking empty cartridge cases sharply against one-another in my warm palms like castanets, whispering 'Stupid soldiers' to myself and promising the scented air that I wouldn't wear nylon stockings next term, or a bra. As the haymakers scythed towards the end of August, my games retreated up the garden, past the sunflowers and the apple tree, on to the terrace, where I acted out stories and sang hymns tunelessly and drove my mother to the brink of lunacy.

'So all day long the noise of battle roll'd' I'd declaim, standing in a rain of blue and yellow caterpillars with the sound of firing bouncing and bumping off the slopes above me. I liked Tennyson because I could swing my legs to him and cry at the same time, and I preferred Gareth and Lynette to the children from the next farm, who jumped out of their hayloft on to a barn floor shining wickedly with pitch forks and scythes, for dares. Childhood was going, going, gone, rushing through my fingers like the earwigs and earth when I dug potatoes, dwindling like the sanity of our landlady as she talked to the slugs under the lettuces, and speeding towards me was the frightening darkness of the rest of my life.

'The years of discretion,' said my form mistress, touching my forehead as she straightened my veil the day I was confirmed. My emotional parent sobbed throughout the service, but perhaps she just didn't like to see the church getting its hooks in me.

'Didn't the landlady have a cousin with a house near

the sawmill?' I asked, struggling up. 'We could go and see if she's still alive. She was a sweet old thing.'

'She'd be over ninety,' said my mother doubtfully, 'and she didn't get on with her son-in-law.' But this life-shortening friction had failed to snuff the old girl out, and she was sitting by the pump shelling peas when we found her.

'Ladies! Ladies!' she called, waving a handful of empty pea pods. 'Where is the little girl?' She had mistaken me for my aunt, and dwelt happily in a past where I was always ten years old. We couldn't make her understand that the little girl and I were the same person, and settled for a curiously cross-eyed conversation in which people rose and fell, now young, now old, now dead, and the chalet existed as it used to be, shining and perfumed with beeswax and woodsmoke, the shutters folded back each morning over scuttling long-legged spiders, the rooms a riot of kittens dressed mercilessly in dolls' clothes, the garden a clear weedless pattern where my mother bent easily to cut chives and shouted at me for picking the scabs off my knees.

We travelled back to Interlaken in the swaying train, eating strawberries out of a crumpled paper punnet and talking to a woman from Zweilütchinen. I caught her looking at me suspiciously as my German accent lost its sharp edge and took on the rounded local sing-song, but I hadn't meant to mimic her; it was easier than I'd expected to slip back into forgotten habits. We swopped stories about the Mettenberg farmer who sent for a vet if his cow coughed but told his wife to sweat out double pneumonia because doctors were expensive, and the Grindelwald man who rushed to a scene of bloody accident only to check that his motor bike was unmarked, and our landlady's brother who fell into a ravine and was amazingly rescued, leaving his sister inconsolable because his new hat had been left behind. It was a swift and cheerful journey.

That evening, sitting in the hotel bar while the hungry

pianist played remorseless nostalgia and my mother calculated that she could just afford the handbag in th Kneoft if we didn't go to the Jungfraujoch, I realised the holiday would soon be over. Pimlico was waiting for me, complete with husband, and lowering across the Thames was the pagan temple of Battersea Power Station, throwing up oily smoke into the pallid sky and never pausing in its creation of the smeary waste which settled on our flat and combined with my husband's moulted coat in a defiantly adhesive layer. I rushed out into the hotel gardens to take lungfuls of fresh air while I had the chance, but it was a mistake on several counts: the pearly evening is muck-spreading time in the Bernese Oberland and I was forced to clap my hands over my nose and mouth and reel back to the lobby; on my hurried, unsteady way I cannoned into a baby waiter, crying mysteriously and uncontrollably into a begonia plant, and when I finally reached the room and sat down on the bed feeling hot and awkward and intrusive I discovered that my one good deed had been to provide supper for an entire family of gnats. Prowling and scratching, I totted up the haul we'd accumulated in our brief stay. There was an assortment of reeking cheeses, banished to the balcony where they panted harmlessly at the nasturtiums, three kinds of Kirsch occupied the bottom of the wardrobe with a kilo can of jam and two new pairs of sandals, a Christmas tree six inches high rested on the table in a polythene bag packed with damp moss, several species of gentian and alpine roses were in the bathroom, similarly preserved, kitchen utensils from the Migros stores and enough chocolate to constipate a platoon sat on the cases and we still wanted to visit the baker's on the day of our departure to buy fresh cakes and rolls. The following morning I went out and bought a holdall, but I should have got two.

My husband met us at Heathrow, keeping his collar turned up and pretending not to know who we were until we'd safely passed Customs.

'All right,' he gritted, the sweat glistening on his forehead as he heaved our baggage into the car. 'How much were you over the limit this time?'

'What limit?' asked my mother innocently. (Now you know where I get it from.)

'Never mind about that,' I said. 'What have you been up to while I've been away?' My mother had put her Christmas tree on top of the third bottle of Remy Martin, but I couldn't close my handbag for miniatures and perfume and my husband was sitting behind the wheel softly but audibly thanking God that he hadn't been with me.

'I've been finalising the arrangements,' he growled, succumbing to an airport bus and causing the baggage to clink and slop alarmingly.

'What arrangements?' I was muffled by what had been in my handbag and my mother was fighting her way out of the damp moss.

'I've confirmed that I'll take the job in Germany, I've given notice to quit at the flat, I've met the prospective tenants and sold them our curtains, the packers come in next month and you and I are moving into an hotel while I go through the induction scheme in London.'

'Anything else?' I asked, fishing a miniature out of my cleavage.

'Well . . . Well, we're going!' He almost took his eyes off the road, but he's got this thing about traffic, so he didn't.

'Well, of course,' I said blandly. 'When?'

He put his head down on the wheel and made a gargling sound. 'Somehow I had this idea you'd object,' he groaned.

Chapter Sixteen

I didn't object to going, but I did object to all the hoo-hah of moving out. We started having a whole new species of row, commencing 'Do you really need . . .'

'Do you really need one hundred and eight back numbers of *'The Accountant'*/all these funny pieces of cardboard/a maintenance manual for a Maserati/those old cardigans made for overweight Siamese twins/seven odd socks?'

'Do you really need thirty-seven little bottles, all with a milimetre of make-up in the bottom/those stacks of recipes for things you won't let me eat/these plastic bags/your old love letters?'

I don't suppose he'd have minded so much if they'd been love letters from him.

By way of a change from clinging on to detritus I considered useful, I had a strenuous time filling up refuse sacks with vast quantities of clothes I was too proud to let the packers see. My activities did not go unremarked by my husband, who was moved to comment on the preponderance of knickers.

'Just how many behinds have you got?' he asked belligerently, carrying out the third sack. (He often asks this question, but usually because of the way I get through toilet paper.) 'You're sure you don't wear three pairs at a time?'

I ignored him, but he came back again.

'Isn't there a jumble sale you could give this to?' he wailed, watching me thrust two drawersful of old tights into a straining waste bin.

'Do you want the whole world to know your wife wears pants with the bows torn off and 38 inch see-through bras?' I demanded.

'I would have thought it was a combination to be proud of,' he said, and was hit over the head with a copy of *Smith's Taxation.*

Our belongings were to go into storage for the next few months, but I was less easy to dispose of, and our biggest problem was what to do with me after my husband had left England and before he found a house in Germany. He didn't fancy me spending my days in expensive hotels over there, getting the waiters to peel my grapes and having nothing to do but flirt and shop. No, far better that I stayed in London and went on working until I had a home to come to, he said, and as I loved Soho so much I could move back there and live with my mother until the great call came. I found the bedevilled woman out on her balcony, forking over her alpine plants with unnecessary force, shortly after this edict had been issued.

'I suppose you'll be taking over the kitchen and living on the phone again,' she said crossly, spearing an inoffensive grass stalk and hurling it over into the abyss. 'And what are you going to do about coming home at night?'

'Whatever do you mean?' I gaped. 'I've been coming home at night for years.'

'Yes, but who with? When you were single you came home with people. Then you came home with your husband.' My mother tore out a remnant of clover and banished it over the coping into the echoing street eleven storeys below. 'Now you're not single and you won't have a husband, and you can't come home on your own, it's not decent!' As I've mentioned before, Soho still has its old fashioned mores.

'Don't be silly,' I said faintly, but I did start to worry. There'd be all that business of arranging for taxis, and getting lifts home from parties again, I'd quite forgotten all that. And being the spare female seated next to the rusting bore, and not having anyone to go to the pictures with because nobody seems to like the films I want to see but you can drag your husband to anything if you tell him it arouses you. (My Chartered Accountant will never refuse taking me to a Western because he knows I'm like a limp and exceptionally promiscuous rag afterwards, and you ought to see *him* after a board room drama.)

Suppose being seule in London proved to be a hideous social handicap? Nearly everyone I knew was paired off, licitly or not, and I'd stick out like a bunion, or be left to rot in my chaperoned eyrie. I tried to keep a stiff lower lip but it was difficult, because although for the time being I still had a husband, and the packers, we were living in hotels.

Up 'til then I hadn't stayed in many English hotels, but I have now. Originally we only intended setting up camp in one, but it's amazing how you can be driven to the nomadic life; we kept believing no other hotel could possibly be as bad as the one we were in, and we kept being proved wrong. For a start, there was the unforeseen hazard presented by the language problem.

I'd long been acquainted with the desperate linguistic lunges of quixotic hotel staff abroad, and had struggled through many a menu typed by some tame but xenophobic chimpanzee – Harry Cot Berts, Salty Pulley, Rind Leg, Game Pastry, Beefstake and Eat Everything – or put up a fight in fractured Serbo Croat for a pot of what was rumoured to be coffee, but now the phenomenon had manifested itself on home ground. There'd been a switch from willing, garrulous old Edward who'd superintended the hall for forty-eight years to a sulky, silent Latin or brooding, tongue-tied Turk, neither of whom would part with anything: luggage, food, drink, towels, soap, hot water or words (English words that is).

I suppose that in a few antique, sedate hostelries in the less frequented byways it would still have been possible to find one or two aged but chatty Britishers, arthritic and incapable of shock, who whisked happy passengers up and down in lifts they'd christened with a pet name thirty years before, and who willingly produced liquid sustenance at any hour of the day or night, but in order to be near both our offices we had to stay right in the centre of the West End, and we found that if you looked for such service in the newer, brighter, flimsier concentration camps you looked in vain.

Under the circumstances, which were bad, we changed hotels like we were playing Monopoly, and rebelliously brushed up our polyglot at the same time. My husband said it did him more good than the Institute of Directors' Language Laboratory. Well, take an apparently simple exercise like ringing down for breakfast in the bleary early morning, with a Californian row thundering through from the indefatigable couple next door (we didn't seem to be able to get away from porous walls anywhere).

Fresh to the game, and naïvely thinking the natives were friendly, I made a stab at the nationality of the accent which answered the phone.

'*Quisiera desayuno, por favor,*' I shouted, to make myself heard over the clashings, clangings and smashings at the other end of the line.

'*Si, Senora,*' grated a voice, and then spoiled my small triumph by turning from the receiver and screaming '*Piano*!' at his tormentors.

After that humiliation, I stuck to snarling 'Breakfast for two,' slamming down the phone, and leaving the hotel an hour or two later, still hungry.

'Thank God, the waiter here's Irish,' we rejoiced one evening in our third port of call. 'We can communicate. We may even get what we order.' But a request for Avocado Vinaigrette brought a scalped avocado and a bottle of vinegar, and my husband's lunatic craving for lasagne resulted in a lengthy, silent study of the menu and a laborious letter-by-letter transcription on to the order pad. The waiter brought canelloni and then stood watching through the portholes in the kitchen doors while a forkful was tasted. It was a mistake my husband didn't make again.

We drank a great deal, when we could, because someone told us alcohol dulls your taste buds, and after ten days of hotel living my spouse got into the habit of presenting himself at the bar at 6.30 p.m. and setting about total anaesthesia before braving the dining-room. All dealings with such emissaries as housekeepers, porters, laundry maids and receptionists he left to me. I had to have a board under my mattress because of my uncooperative spine and I did not thank the Lord my God for leaving me to explain this wherever we went. At one link in the caravanserai-chain, a defensive French receptionist came up to the room with me, bringing a Spanish porter, and we had a council of war.

'Before we get too involved,' I said cautiously. 'I'd like to point out that we only have one set of towels for two people.' The receptionist refused to use the house phone (and I could hardly blame her) and turned to the porter.

'Serviettes,' she snapped peremptorily.

'Hostia puta,' he countered, amiably enough.

Shaken rigid but hoping she hadn't spent as much time in Spain as I had, I explained to the porter that we made a lack of *toallas*, and he said he would speak to the housekeeper. He added that the housekeeper came from Alicante, and he came from Campello, and we had a *paeso* down memory lane while the French girl throbbed with impatience and jangled her bracelets at us.

'Oh, and I need a board,' I said hastily, 'to put under the mattress.'

The porter eyed me cynically and enquired whether I'd tried lying down yet. Feeling self-conscious, I stretched out on the bed while they stood watching me.

'It's all right, I don't need a board after all,' I admitted.

Exit staff. Their florid exchanges echoed all the way down the corridor and through the tissue door, and did my ego no good.

At the next hotel, the spirited Italian who helped us

with our cases (he held the door open for us while we carried them in) could not be made to see what was wrong with my concave bed. After a nightmare half-hour which ended with him bursting into tears and my husband striding out in search of gin, I nervously lifted the telephone receiver and was informed by a sad Swede that 'Evry bort in the hows is ocupite'. Visions of commercial travellers on boards, conventions on boards, grandmas and grandpas on boards, honeymooners on boards, tarts on boards and tots on boards floated before my eyes. The Italian had a short conversation with the disembodied Swede, but no common ground was reached. He did revive sufficiently to make a pass at me before he left, but as he'd also made a pass at my husband in the foyer, I didn't feel I could derive much that was complimentary from the experience.

I wandered the two inches to the window, fought the

double glazing, lost, and gloomed down at the streets of London far beneath me. There were English people out there, talking to one-another, ordering beer and double gins, getting papers, *eating*. Thin walls did not a prison make, I would go out.

Forty-five minutes later, when I had established that one lift did not work, the second only went up, the third was occupied by a restive and growing crowd of Americans who kept trying to get to the ground floor but couldn't make it and the fourth was crammed with class-conscious staff, I was back in the room again. My husband was waiting for me, his speech strangely slurred. Pacing around the corridors, he'd found a desperately friendly man from Georgia carrying an engraved hip flask and a packet of Graham Crackers. They'd spent quite some time sitting on a banquette, drinking and watching the lifts, and the Southerner ventured to comment that he hadn't been able to get out and eat for a day and a half.

'All human life is there,' my husband said solemnly, gesturing at a lift, and his new friend remarked that lifts had fascinated him ever since he was a child. When he was about eight he was taken to a large store in Macon one Christmas and had stood with his mother, waiting to enter one of the capacious lifts and travel up to the toy department. The doors flexed open, the crowd bulged and dragged, and his mother exclaimed wisely 'We'll never get in there,' yanking him back beside her. A scrawny, agile lady who'd been standing nearby obviously judged that if they weren't going in, there might be room for her, leapt forward as the steel doors were closing and was neatly decapitated. Her head fell within the lift, her body slithered to the carpet outside, the lift operator swung on the brakes of his conveyance with such energy that he jammed it between floors, and a pregnant lady passenger became hysterical and started to give birth. It was nearly three hours before engineers got the lift down and the people out, and the post natal lady told newspapermen she'd be calling her daughter Julie, which was an old family name.

My husband and the Southern gentleman sat in silence for a little while after the unfolding of this tale, and contemplated the empty flask. When they parted, it was with courteous promises that should either of them find a means of egress from the hotel he would inform the other. My husband even suggested walking down, but he had forgotten by then what floor they were on and was shaken to his lethargic core when reminded.

'Thanks for coming back,' I sniffed. I felt deprived, not having bumped into a gentleman with a hip flask since the day I got married, and salt tears lapped at my mascara. The returned explorer patted me in a conciliatory manner, giving rise to what we both thought was a good idea, and we determined instantly to take solace in one of the few human activities to which lack of room service is no bar. Unfortunately, we were more enthusiastic than discreet and abruptly discovered that some temporarily untenanted boards had been purloined and lovingly placed under our mattresses while we'd been away.

Dinner consisted of a sandwich taken standing up at a snack counter, and was followed by a chaste night, the silence of which was broken by an occasional moan or wince.

'It won't be like this in Germany,' promised a sorrowful voice in the darkness. 'You can come over to visit me as soon as I've lined up some properties, and perhaps we'll have a decent night's . . . Well, some edible food.'

'Hah!' I said. My 'Hahs' are widely known and devastating. I still hadn't forgiven him for leaving me chained to a desk in London while he house-hunted and set things up in Deutschland, and neither had my mother. After all, it must be a bit of a blow having your difficult daughter dumped back in your lap when your blood pressure's barely down to normal again after getting rid of her.

So at the end of the summer I bade my husband a

frosty farewell and moved into my mother's flat. I wrote long mournful letters and short salacious articles in my celibate evenings, to pass the time between white hot culinary disagreements, and received short cheerful letters and small cheques in return. The money at least was encouraging, but it was a peculiar life, neither one thing nor the other (definitely not the other) and I looked forward to the first of my flying visits to my spouse, not least for the pleasures of the Duty Free Shop. There wouldn't be all that long to wait, and in the meantime there were some intriguing and hitherto unsuspected sidelights of my mother's life with which to occupy my mind. She'd become a member of the Regent's Park club.

Chapter Seventeen

My family had enjoyed a long association with the park. On fine days when I was a baby my mother used to put me and her sewing in a pram and trundle up Portland Place, and I'd sit cooing and gurgling on the grass while she hunched in a deckchair finishing a vicuna coat for some gentleman of property or other. No wonder she's got back trouble now; deckchairs are so exceedingly unversatile.

A lawn near the Open Air Theatre was a rendezvous for mothers, the more practical of whom festooned the box hedges with drying bibs and nappies, and if approached by a pompous keeper, my parent defended any and every maternal activity with that useful phrase 'There's a war on!', returning to her stitching with such determination that she was left undisturbed.

When I was older, I went to a school near Regent's Park, and my cronies and I used to go for walks there in our lunch hours, beret-ed heads close together, discussing who'd achieved a French kiss yet. Even on the coldest days the park was preferable to the playground, and we gladly suffered the attentions of those poor exhibitionists who risked frostbite rather than miss the chance of unzipping themselves on some lonely path before a nubile bunch of uniformed schoolgirls. Discounting the boring and somewhat stunted exhibitionists, the park was always interesting, and provided us with the privacy we needed to debate biology, a topic of which we never tired and which filled us with mingled excitement and dread. We were also fascinated by our teachers' love affairs and hoped the Maths' mistress's temper would improve after her impending marriage, as it was understood that the reasons for her homicidal rages could be looked for in the frustrations of her interminable engagement. I remember that we read and discussed Freud and Biggles with equal ardour and puzzlement, and I never dared tell anyone that, having studied a book on dream interpretation in which it was suggested that suitcases could represent the genital parts of strangers, my sleep was thronged for weeks by husky porters who carried everything from attaché cases to cabin trunks.

After I'd left school and started work, I neglected the park. It was too far away to be reached for lunch time walks, and at week-ends I disdained its blandishments and risked every possible disaster, swallowing travel pills and trustingly climbing into motor cars to disappear into the country for what my mother thought was fresh air. It was incredible how near the country got to the town sometimes, especially when I took notice of the sunshine on the calendar, defied my own thermostat and wore shorts or plunging necklines. I was lucky if I reached Hampstead Heath before the driver complained of hunger and thirst and commented that here was as nice a place to pull up as any. What he pulled up I discovered to my cost.

It was with renewed interest after an absence of years that I reverted to Regent's Park when I got married, and dragged my husband round and round the perimeter every Sunday for the sake of our health. We could have gone farther afield, but my travel sickness, the congestion on the roads and my pathological reaction to wild life such as ants beyond the suburbs convinced my spouse that there was insufficient reason to add more to the mileage total he notched up on business during the course of the week. We were both content to have the wide open spaces so near at hand, and made preparations for trips to the park as thoroughly as if we were going on Safari.

Since childhood I've had a mania for picnics, which I used to eat on the roof of our first chicken and eunuch infested flat in Kingly Street, and was given to summer tantrums when I assembled precarious bagfuls of food and demanded to be taken somewhere where I could eat and breathe at the same time. Since I could be so easily satisfied in Queen Mary's Rose Garden, my husband saw no need to prolong the agonies of transit, and we spent many fairly amiable hours on old blankets, listening to the music of the band.

The band was a Sunday afternoon happening which occurred between Spring and Autumn. The Royal Artillery or Kodak or some other worthy body would despatch to the Inner Circle a glistening charabanc of round-cheeked, wide-eyed brass bandsmen, who set up their little music stands on the lawn near the boating lake and played selections from Strauss and Gilbert and Sullivan or, greatly daring, Henry Mancini and John Barry. On gusty days the sound travelled considerable distances and might reach us near the rain gauge or the ornamental island, and it was pleasant to wander down to the lake and watch the musicians fighting with their sheet music as the wind sucked and blew. I was made happy for hours by such simple diversions as the band striking up *Raindrops Keep Falling On My Head* in a sudden shower. Small and uncontrolled children went and rested their chins on the music stands, staring with disconcerting intensity into the faces of the buglers, and obnoxious, flirtatious little girls stood right under the conductor's armpits and were trodden back upon with malicious accuracy and obvious satisfaction. Practically the only times I didn't quarrel with my husband were when we had our mouths full or were listening to music, so picnics near the band did much for our marriage.

What I didn't appreciate until I moved back to Soho was the part which Regent's Park had come to play in my mother's life. Both she and the meek aunt were retired now, and the only boss for whom they stitched and tacked was me. Under the guidance of a brilliant, endlessly patient and endlessly harried dress designer friend of mine, my mother attempted garments of awful complexity and terrific chic, when I caught her, but officially speaking her time was her own, and she and my aunt patrolled the park daily, regarding it as Soho's grounds. Their familiarity with the landscape was to be expected, but the vast number and diversity of their acquaintance amongst the other habitués took me by surprise.

'I wonder whether we'll see the duck lady,' my mother said, the first Sunday of my grass widowhood, as we boarded a 53 bus in Regent Street.

'No, she's gone to Eastbourne,' responded my aunt. 'The pigeon woman told me.'

Thus I was introduced to the code of the park club, which required complete anonymity of anyone over 45. The widows, the spinsters and those who were neither, met and talked and fed their favourite birds or animals, but never exchanged names – it just wasn't done. Not unnaturally, the obvious need for descriptive adjectives didn't always result in flattery.

'The duck lady,' for instance, not only devoted her exclusive attentions to the ducks, whom she'd christened and knew one from another by differences of beak or web or squawk which would have been lost on anyone else, but also because she looked very much like a duck herself. Similarly, the pigeon lady had an enormous frontage and a habit of setting back her head and blinking rapidly, and I was all agog to meet someone called the leopard woman until it turned out that she merely wore a leopardskin coat.

The flower man was a dear little suntanned soul who carefully tucked abandoned, wind-blown blossoms into his buttonhole, a bunch at a time, so that he could be recognised from a great distance by the colours decorating his dark raincoat. He carried all his possessions with him in a shopping bag because, he confided, it wasn't safe to leave them where he spent his nights.

Those without obvious distinquishing marks were designated by nationality – the Portuguese lady, the French woman and the Austrian man – or the place in which they lived – The White House lady and the Rowton House man.

Having assimilated these basic rules of the club, I thought the most difficult hurdle was cleared and Sunday walks with my mother could be taken in peaceful co-existence, but my initiation had hardly begun. Seeing a squirrel clinging to a tree trunk at the end of the Broad Walk, I approached it with an outstretched nut and was snatched back by my mother as though I'd stepped into a circle of fire.

'Stop it at once,' she cried excitedly. 'This is the Belgian lady's tree.'

'What on *earth* . . .' I gasped.

'Come along quickly, before she sees you,' urged my parent. 'Do hurry up. Oh, thank goodness, she was telling off a tourist and didn't notice us. I don't know what I could have said if she'd caught you.'

By means of this and other bewildering conversations, I gathered that each club member fed a particular specie in a particular part of the park, and guarded their pitches as jealously as buskers. There was, in fact, a certain show business element involved, most noticeably in the summer when crowds of tourists and out-of-towners came to the Zoo. The lady or gentleman with a spot in the Broad Walk was then much envied. They nearly all had a polished routine, with a short monologue to deliver, and a typical entertainment started like this: the performer, striding briskly past other pitches, would halt with dramatic suddenness a few yards from his or her tree, and stand gazing at it, not with the brimming admiration for nature which the art students affected, nor with the curiosity of the visiting Americans, many of whom remarked generously that the trees in our parks were unusually free from graffiti. No, this gaze was measured and intense. It sought something and found it.

'Ah!' the pitch-holder would shout exultantly. '*There* you are!'

At this piercing cry, people unfamiliar with the Broad

Walk performances would often pause in their strolling and look round. With perfect timing, the park member would then step closer to the tree and stretch out a hand, or a little bag, or even a hat, and a minimum of three squirrels would erupt from in and around the trunk. Next would follow some banter with the intrigued onlookers before the tit-bits were distributed, but from this point on the acts differed in content and quality. One man was such a professional that he could keep a crowd happy for hours; squirrels ran up and down his legs and dived head first inside his jacket, and one even used to take off his trilby. There was also a bit of business with a waste bin.

At the other end of the bill, meanness or over-caution could result in a poor act, for the squirrels would spit out stale nuts, or sit on their hind legs squittering in complaint at unsatisfactory rations, and the watchers were quick to tumble an entertainer who attempted to drag out his act by breaking up peanuts and relinquishing them an eighth at a time.

Usually the performances were short, and relied for their success on the fine judgement with which the pitch-holders went to have a sit down and a rest between shows, until there had been a change of house, as it were, before they started again.

Sometimes an entertainer worked from a bench, but these performers had to have great experience and panache, for the limitations of their sedentary position meant that they stood or fell by the star quality of the fauna they managed to attract.

My mother and aunt, being relative newcomers to park membership, roamed widely and took uncomplicated pleasure in feeding the ducks by the ornamental lake (an unscheduled territory as it supported too much passing trade to be kept exclusive), or the promiscuous sparrows near the rose bushes. It was when I was standing waiting near the rose bushes one day, clutching a bag of crusts for the ducks, that I became aware of my mother's kleptomania. Pausing in her sparrow fostering, she peered at a clump of lavender and bent to nip some off.

'You can't do that!' I exclaimed, feeling it was my turn to be scandalised.

'You ought to see me in the spring,' laughed my mother, quite unashamed and taking deep sniffs at the lavender crushed between her fingers. 'Haven't you noticed all that privet on my balcony? And the gardeners gave me a whole lot of geraniums they were turfing out last week.'

A little suspicious and uncertain, I walked on beside the floraphile. Mounds of peat were stacked along the paths, waiting to refurbish the flower beds, and my parent actually licked her lips.

'If only I had a carrier,' she whispered.

'You don't mean you take earth as well?' I asked.

'Yes, of course,' she said impatiently. 'When there's something handy to put it in. And stop looking at me like that, I've only got a few window boxes, not a market garden.'

We skirted more peat and found a group of gardeners, toiling uphill on the remaking of an awkward stretch, and an extremely elegant lady who had approached from the opposite direction and was now standing on tiptoe trying to avoid soiling her crocodile shoes on the damp grass.

'Hello, there,' she called delicately, flapping a calf-clad hand. 'Hello, gardener!'

A young man pushed his plait out of his eyes and tramped down the hillside. 'Yeah?' he said.

'No, I want to speak to a *gardener*,' said the stylish lady firmly, her idea of a gardener obviously being someone over fifty with short hair. The youth struggled back up the hill again and after a few minutes an older man clumped down. I was reminded of ladies in chemist's who must speak to a female assistant, and started to giggle into my bag of crusts. The gardener asked what he could do for her and the crocodile lady shot me a glare and bent as close as she dared to the mould-spattered worker.

'I'd like some earth,' she breathed into his ear. Then, gathering courage: 'Some nice *leafy* earth.' She looked rather excited.

'Right you are then, my dear,' said the gardener. 'Got your bag handy, have you?'

Blushing like a girl, the lady produced a folded up shopping bag and stood trembling with pleasure while the receptacle was filled and handed back.

'It's amazing the people with window boxes these days,' confided my mother, as we walked on towards the tea house. 'Did you see her shoes?'

I can remember when the tea house was pre-war Tudor in appearance and did a brisk trade in ices, but time's chariot wheels had ground over the old building and a spiky arrangement called a restaurant had shot up in its place, presided over by the ubiquitous Mr Forte, who was actually prepared to dispense strong drink during licensing hours. With the waning of the summer and the crowds, I grew to like this place more and more; there was time to chat, and on cold days you could sit inside and drink coffee in comfort, watching the wet winds hurl plastic spoons and biscuit wrappers at the windows.

I was interested to note how my hotel-based observations were applicable to the tea house, which ran on palm-oiled wheels but sometimes failed to conceal the usual multi-national problems behind its pseudo-Yank façade. One Sunday lunch time, two hapless French couples sat down at a table near me and were instantly ordered off by the only waitress then in evidence, a plump young Greek girl.

'There is no service at that table,' she squeaked crossly. The obedient French people arose and reformed elsewhere. They then attempted to summon the waitress to take their order.

'I don't serve at that table,' she squealed, and vanished. There were no other empty tables, and the French people looked non-plussed.

I was sitting by the entrance to the kitchen and could hear the row going on inside.

'I will not go out there,' howled a masculine voice which I could only classify as middle-European. 'I do not serve frogs! Frog-eaters! I hate them. Let them eat the menus!'

The Greek girl reappeared with my fruit salad. 'He's Polish,' she giggled to me, planking down my bowl, 'and he's never forgiven the French for the way his girl friend left him for a dish-washer from Toulouse.'

'A *mechanical* dish-washer?' I asked.

The French couples got up again and went away. They must have been fairly quick on the uptake, or perhaps they'd been staying in London for some time.

Although I wasn't eligible for full membership myself, I liked visiting my mother's outdoor club. The décor was changed regularly, it never got stuffy, there was sufficient space and undergrowth to hide in if you saw someone coming whom you didn't like, and a wide range of interests was catered for, from kleptomania and masochism (there were track-suited individuals who thumped round the Inner Circle thirty-eight times before breakfast) to self-exposure.

Gradually I became acquainted with the younger set, who did exchange names and even telephone numbers, but they and my mother's group were purely on nodding terms. There was a beautiful young actress who looked like an advert for yeast pills and walked in the park sniffing the roses between jobs, numerous dog and children exercisers, and rabid footballers who would have played equally well without a ball.

Occasionally I wondered whether I too shouldn't be doing something hearty, but mostly I wandered about staring at the trees and telling myself nature was a calming influence. The serenity of the park was welcome, for a little worry was niggling away at the back of my mind.

Chapter Eighteen

It was when I was doing some Saturday shopping, shortly before flying over to see my husband, that the idea hit me – right between the ovaries you might say. I looked absently at the pots of jam lined up on the check-out counter (apricot, damson, black cherry, three types of marmalade) and a deep suspicion (why are suspicions never shallow?) formed in my fertile mind.

'Could this be pregnancy?' I wondered, handing over a note and being told rather coldly that one pound was not enough. 'And why do I like such expensive preserves?' The second thought had nothing to do with the first, but was valid as a piece of self-interrogation.

Wandering back through Soho with the bag of jam jars clasped in my arms and doing irreparable harm to my uplift bra, I hoped that I was merely having another outbreak of gluttony, like the chopped herring and smoked salmon jag I used to go on in Pimlico whenever I was homesick, or my ruinous Beluga and lobster kick. The latter was cut off in its prime when my husband, complete with the bank statement from which he is so rarely separable, made it clear that if my expensive craving weren't short-lived, I would be.

The trouble with me is that I can never be sure whether it's greed or pregnancy I'm suffering from. I'm always developing strange gastronomic longings, rushing out to buy a couple of tons of my fancy and then stopping dead in my tracks with my armloads of whatever, struck by the thought that there might be a good old fashioned reason for my actions. And it's a waste of time getting out my diary and trying to remember things like my twenty-eight-times table, because after hours of calculations and guess work all I get is a headache and remarkably few crosses on the calendar. The problem is hardly new.

When I was in my doomful teens our aged G.P. would look at me over his spectacles and tell me I was irregular.

'Irregular you are and irregular you'll stay,' was how he put it. 'Something up with your endocrines, probably, but you look perfectly all right to me.'

And I did look all right. As I only had a visitation once a Quarter at most, I went spotty and tearful so infrequently nobody noticed, and there's no denying you don't get pre-menstrual tension unless you're going to be menstrual. But our dear old G.P. had no idea what my black teenage imagination made of these vicissitudes.

'Can this be pregnancy?' was a question I started asking myself, and went on asking myself, from the moment I discovered it didn't mean having crooked teeth.

There was a great deal of publicity and speculation about virgin birth when I was fourteen, and having read myself into a terrible state of nerves I used to turn sideways and study my rounded stomach in any mirror that was handy, dolefully convinced I was mug enough to have been honoured by the Holy Ghost and slept through the whole thing. Something always turned up, it's true, but it usually turned up with sadistic ferocity on special occasions like the first day of the holidays, when parthenogenesis wasn't in the forefront of my mind.

As I grew older, the question I posed myself became somewhat more realistic. During one of my engagements, I went and stormed at the doctor that I didn't intend to be subjected to a pregnancy test every month of my life, and he tutted and muttered about 'settled emotions' and 'fulfilment' and 'motherhood' (he had a touchingly antique view of wedlock). However, he sent me off on a round of consultations that would have satiated the libido of Catherine the Great. During the weeks that followed I devoured boxes of pills, gloomily studied the balding pates of countless specialists wavering between my knees, and learned after all that I was incorrigibly irregular, but should be consoled because my womb was quite perfect, with just the right degree of tilt.

'Positively inviting conception,' said one gynaecologist smugly, throwing me into a state of panic unequalled since the days of my virgin-birth syndrome. I went around covered from head to foot in thick hand-knit wool (luckily it was winter) and had terrible visions that my mother's friends' 'He only has to throw his trousers on my bed' type comments were based in fact. If my womb was running amuck, inviting conception, what (apart from tying my knees together) could I do? It took a long time for those particular mental scars to heal, and I still have nightmares in which my roquish womb is leaning over a four ale bar winking at likely impregnators.

Contrary to naïve expectations, the elusive character of my curse developed rather than diminished with the years. When the Chartered Accountant I was to marry remarked one evening that I was exceptionally even tempered ('even', notice, not 'good'), so much so that he could never tell when I had a period, I replied casually that it was hardly surprising seeing I hadn't had one for six months. I didn't think I'd ever bring him round. He swore he'd never get used to it, and he hasn't. No more have I. It's become known as the Scarlet Pimpernel in our home. And during the past summer, just to add complications to the issue, my husband had gone through a brief but terrifyingly intense broody phase, declaring himself determined somehow, some time, somewhere to get me pregnant. I don't know whether he was worried at the thought of leaving me alone in London or simply couldn't face the sight of another Wellington, but whichever it was, his master plan certainly wrought some changes in the months prior to his departure.

Up to then he'd always been a Do-It-Yourself man – you know, ask him to help you with anything and he'd grunt 'Do it yourself' – but he made an exception in this instance, no matter how strenuously or how often I put forward the virgin birth possibility.

As may be evident, I didn't go broody with him, and manoeuvring me into a maternal frame of mind wasn't an easy matter, although my husband made many a gallant try at it. 'Could do better' is the sort of end of term report phrase that springs to mind. Dry-eyed when shown round Mothercare, I failed utterly to mist over at the sight of a pattern for woolly bootees, and my husband left England resigned to the idea that motherhood would only result from a sudden surprise attack or a stroke of fate. At one time he'd pinned rather a lot of faith on a corn dolly, and even hard hearted and joyfully unfertilised I felt a twinge of sympathy for him over that pathetic episode.

When we were leading our disruptive hotel existence, and moaning about it to anyone who would listen, a well-meaning but unworldly friend sent us a corn dolly, with a covering note explaining its significance as a good-luck bringer and efficacious fertility symbol. Needless to say, the friend was more my husband's than mine.

I was afraid to touch the beastly thing, but Broody went potty with delight and took pains to append the corn dolly from a convenient light fitting or television aerial wherever we unpacked and prepared to spend yet another sleepless night. Since he'd somehow got the idea that in order to maximise the effect the ritual object should be suspended directly above the centre of operations, ours was not an easy row to hoe. Well, have you *seen* where they tuck light fittings nowadays?

Even when we infrequently came across a conventional room with an ordinary, outmoded lamp in the middle of the ceiling, there was a debit side to the short-lived relief. Despite its open accessibility, I couldn't wait until my husband had started snoring, put my gloves on and then climb up and cut the dolly down, because I suffer from vertigo. The nights I lay there, plotting ways to mangle the dreadful thing to pulp . . .

I told my friends about it and no one would come up and have a drink with us any more, for fear of contributing to ecological disaster. In fact life was so fraught I was twanging, when the Scarlet Pimpernel put in an unannounced and abrupt reappearance exactly four weeks to the day since I'd last bade it farewell. My opinion of corn dollies and my husband's well-meaning chums underwent a dramatic reversal, and it was an awful moment when I skipped out of the bathroom all happy and glowing and found my husband grimly shredding his fertility symbol into the bowl of cereal on our breakfast tray (which had been delivered by mistake), but at least we could start going to bed in bed again, and I no longer had to listen to cries of 'Wait a minute, down a bit, now edge towards the wardrobe!'

Resting my chin on the carrier bag and fishing for my door keys, I worked out that it was nearly three months since the dolly had been despatched to eternal rest, and the Scarlet Pimpernel showed no signs of a repeat performance in the near future. Added to which I was eating enough jam for a family of six. I stood considering, and trying to remember whether my bosom was on the move, and in which direction. There really wasn't any point in fretting for at least another seven weeks, although it would be typical of the way I mismanaged things if I'd got pregnant when my husband was well out of his paternal patch. He was being exposed to other people's children in Germany, and the tone of his letters was about as fatherly as W. C. Fields.

'Perhaps air travel will stir things up,' I thought, brightening, 'it usually does. And then there's all that bending and stretching when I pack.'

The forthcoming visit to my panting partner assumed an even happier role in my mind, and I quite forgot to worry when I started fancying smoked eel.

Chapter Nineteen

Although I would have preferred being frisked by a man, being examined for concealed weapons is a stimulating sensual experience, and I boarded the plane in a pleasant state of excitement. I really do love flying, even when there's nothing therapeutic to be expected from it, and most of all I love taking off. I get this fantastic feeling of exhilaration just sitting strapped into my seat. There's the way the aircraft starts throbbing under you, sending gorgeous impulses up your back and other places, and I always wear trousers for flying so I can sit with my legs apart and not cause comment.

The Trident sat on its coccyx and leapt into the air, and I gave a happy little shriek of delight (what a blessing are half empty flights) and ordered myself a drink. I had an idea I might need it. Of course, my husband had achieved a life-long ambition in going to a country where there was such a thing as a cheap drunk, and was revelling in it, but I didn't know much about Lower Saxony except that it sounded as though the natives went about in those helmets with horns on. Then I couldn't help wondering whether life in Germany would have changed him. We hadn't seen each other for ages and we'd got on badly enough before, but it was rather urgent (I shifted about in my seat) that in some basic respects he should have stayed the same. I spent the rest of the flight drinking, feeling randy, eyeing the other passengers so blatantly that they huddled together for protection, and making trips to the loo to see if anything had happened (it hadn't).

At Hanover I fell down the steps of the aeroplane and

was helped up by a steward who reeled back when I breathed. Hoping my mirror hadn't shattered, I tottered across the tarmac and through Customs, and there was this friendly-looking, portly chap, shouting and waving at me.

'Who's he?' I puzzled blearily. 'I don't know him, do I?' But the rotund gentleman was behaving in a very informal way, and he tasted familiar. 'It's *you*!' I spluttered.

'Aren't you wearing your contact lenses?' asked my husband's voice.

'You bet I'm wearing my contact lenses,' I spat. 'And I wish I wasn't. What's happened to you?'

'Oh, I've put on a pound or two,' he beamed. 'The beer over here . . .'

'Don't tell me,' I said. 'Don't tell me. You realise this will affect our whole way of life?' With which penetrating reference to our researches in the field of human contact I went to find the car, leaving my husband to cope with my luggage, which weighed almost as much as he did. On my way to the parking area, I passed two bookstalls covered with magazines whose covers proclaimed in large, multi-coloured letters *'Dick ist schön'* ('Fat is beautiful'). From the look at my husband and the local population, this was no news, and my worse half soon made it clear that he hadn't enjoyed himself so much since he was accidentally locked in a Santa's Fairy Grotto at the age of five. After a year and a half of a bullying wife who counted his calories as though every single unit had to be dug out of her own spleen, and spat blood when asked to provide gin with her housekeeping money, he was experiencing such glories of freedom that he hardly noticed an inconvenience or two (apart from celibacy, but he'd had some training for that on our honeymoon). All right, so his working day started at 8. a.m. instead of 9.30 – the land was flowing with Eisbein and Sauerkraut, and Niersteiner Domtal was something you used to water the garden.

As we bored along the autobahns, I watched ice forming

on the inside of the windows and promised myself that next time I flew over I'd put on at least two more layers of woolly everything before I stepped out of the plane. Nothing that wasn't subcutaneous could insulate me against such cold as this, but I'd freeze to death trying.

'Puh. Puh-puh,' I stuttered.

'Wha-wha?' queried my old man (the frost had given him a white beard).

'Puh-puh. *Pull*,' I managed to emit through juddering teeth, jabbing a frozen finger at a distant food and drink sign. Miraculously my message was received and understood, and we pulled up and thawed out at the next service station. All around us in the steamy haze of condensation, chubby folk tucked into slithering mountains of food. The sight and the aroma made the saliva gush down my throat, but I wanted to fit into my clothes just a little longer and decided to wait to eat, at least until dinner time. My husband had a three-course snack.

Later that evening, when he was trying to separate me from some of my clothing, I told him I had never been so cold, but he'd had months to acclimatise and he thought I was joking when I said I intended sleeping in my fur coat. I turned the central heating up so high it chugged, and spent the night listening to my husband's forgotten snores and longing for my mother's stone hot water bottle.

During the days that followed, I came to understand that although the winter weather in Northern Germany makes England look like a sub-tropical paradise, only the expatriate English find the climate worthy of discussion; we may talk about the weather but the Germans have weightier things on their minds: they discuss food. And what food! German women expect to be shown the family tree of every cutlet before they buy it, boycott unsatisfactory or slipshod butchers until they go bankrupt, regard packaged convenience foods as the last desperate resort of blind paraplegics, and have a schnapps for every occasion.

I staggered under the impact of the hospitality I was

offered, but then I'm a Londoner and we're not renowned for the alacrity with which we open our doors to strangers. 'Oh, Christ, Chateau D'If!' my husband used to groan, as we stood outside my mother's front door and listened to her unlatching, unbolting, unchaining and preparing to repel boarders. In contrast to this reserved modus vivendi, I found that visiting anyone in Germany (even to have a key cut) meant being dragged from the hall into the living-room, tucked into the most comfortable chair and proffered coffee, wine, brandy and cakes the size of the Great Bed of Ware; there was always the chance that an entire hour might have elapsed since your last meal. After a few half-hearted attempts to retain some semblance of a waistline, I promised myself to fast when I got back to London and became a gluttonous enthusiast about the whole thing. Within three days I couldn't see my ribs any more, my husband stopped trying to hold his breath and his stomach in when he undressed, and I stopped telling him off every time he looked at a potato.

'If I make up my mind to lie back and enjoy it,' I thought, 'Germany could be fun.' Unfortunately, some other expatriate wives I met were not so keen to unknot their moral fibre, and were finding adjustment to the Hun a sticky business. This was particularly true of the Army wives, whose husbands hadn't freely chosen the new homeland, and who longed for the good old days in Aldershot, when milk was delivered to the door in bottles and sausages were recognisable short, fat things that you fried. A major factor in the alienation from which they suffered appeared to be their lack of knowledge of the German language, and I thanked God nightly for the urge to talk which had prompted me to equip myself for conversation abroad. I couldn't have borne being unable to talk to people just because they weren't English, and from an early age I made the appropriate preparations. The Swiss holidays probably had a lot to do with it too; I used to play with other vacationing children and refused to be put off if they spoke French, German or Italian.

Whilst it was easy to understand the predicament of a recently uprooted wife, newly arrived and loath to tote Langenscheidt round to the supermarket with her, I was amazed at the apathy of the expatriates who were still at the shout and mime stage after many years in Germany, and who were content to isolate themselves from the native population indefinitely rather than tussle with absurd old grammar. No wonder there were a few degrees of frost on Anglo-German relations in the areas so thronged with British Army personnel; the Germans thought the English were stilted and unfriendly when they were merely inhibited and scared of being done, and the English thought the Germans were laughing at them, when they were only laughing at the small quantities they ate.

Although my husband's appetite insured him against derision, it was over a menu that his relationship with colloquial Deutsch came unstuck. He hadn't had a go at the language since his schooldays, and was rather proud of the progress he'd made, glibly slipping the odd double-taxation or currency movement reference into any conversation, until I testily reminded him that what he was saying would have been incomprehensible to me in English. I'd got quite huffy at his expertise, I'm ashamed to admit. I used to be the one who was good at languages, and now his complicated commercial vocabulary put him unarguably one up.

We were stomping round the grounds of the Schloss in Celle, puffing on our fingers and debating which builder to visit next, when I realised with horror that my ego must plumb a new low.

'I've even forgotten the word for duck,' I wailed. 'I wanted to ask about those ducks on the moat and I couldn't remember the word.'

'Easy,' crowed my husband. '*Spiegel, der Spiegel.*'

'*Spiegel* is a mirror,' I said quickly, beginning to feel a warming glow in my self-esteem once more. 'Haven't you seen that news magazine?'

'Oh, well, of course it may mean mirror too,' he condescended, doggedly going on to destruction. 'It could be one of those words that mean two things, but you must have noticed duck eggs on all the menus.'

'Never,' I breathed innocently. 'Never in my life.'

'Of course you have,' he said crossly, '*Spiegel Eier*. They're everywhere. Can't understand why they're so popular, I wouldn't like . . .'

I'm not sure whether he stopped talking or I drowned the rest of the sentence, but I was laughing so much I nearly fell in the moat.

'*Spiegel Eier*,' I gasped, 'are fried eggs! It's a colloquialism. Did you think that magazine was called *The Duck of the World*?'

'Well, I . . .' he wavered.

'It'll be good news for Bonn,' I said.

I was enormously bucked by this conversation and fell about every time I passed a newagent's, gurgling *The Duck of the World*, but I was sufficiently reasonable to admit that he could have made a worse mistake, like the friend who went into a crowded shop and asked for four *Scheisse* of liver when he should have said *Scheibe*.

As we picked our way through newly-built flats and tumbledown farms, and fought off friendly men and their pipelines of cognac and *Steinhager*, we came no nearer to finding a home and I came no nearer to sympathizing with girls I met who complained bitterly that the village plumbers didn't understand plain English. At tea one afternoon with four or five Army wives who'd come rushing to meet me in my capacity as a British subject, I tried to bring the landscape into the conversation, as I was incredibly bored with hearing about the unfriendliness and all round awfulness of the Huns themselves.

'Parts of the country are very beautiful,' I persisted. 'The Black Forest . . .'

'Wales is better,' said someone.

'But Baden-Baden . . .' I began.

'Yes, that's nice,' agreed someone else, reviving, 'You might almost be in England there.'

I gave up and drank my tea. I didn't expect starting life in a new country to be a cakewalk, but did it need to be the death-throes-cum-labour pains these people made out.

A slender lady said she missed the Academy so much and burst in tears, and I was very jarred until it was explained that she meant the Royal Academy and not the cinema in Oxford Street.

'Be positive,' I told myself firmly. 'Pimlico was as congenial as San Quentin, you can't stay in Soho on your mother's divan for ever, and your Chartered Accountant is over here. Every child needs a father.' (Nothing had happened yet.)

My fellow-countrymen remained the greatest disadvantage that Germany had to offer, but I was greatly encouraged when I met a couple of cheerful transplanted freaks who were happy with their new lot. There were also ladies who preferred German shops to the N.A.A.F.I. and others who said they felt like sluts in comparison to the hard working Hausfraus. Sadly, this praise was almost as damning as the actual grumbles, because any mention of immaculate German linen or sparkling German glass or polished German floors was accompanied by a simpering, deprecating smile which implied, and not always mutely, that English women were liberated now and didn't consider housekeeping that important. Funnily enough, while relative levels of domestic skill were frequently chewed over, few liberated expatriate women referred to the cultural, economic or political facets of the society around them, and long afternoons were spent companionably swopping recipes and hints on potty training, rather than studying to be barristers or brushing up their Latin (or even their German). I came to the conclusion that if Englishwomen were slovenly it was because they wanted to be, and not because they were too busy doing liberated things to clean the stove. It was dawning on me that if I wanted to hold my head up in German society, I had some homework as well as some housework to do.

The same Saxon widow who fed and liquored me throughout one afternoon, telling me of her visits to Vienna (dumplings and *Sacher Torte*), Amsterdam (cheese, gin and advocaat), Berne (*rosti*, pear brandy and chocolate) and Paris (ignominiously unstarred), went on in the evening to discuss Grillparzer, Hemingway, Faulkner, Kafka, Shakespeare, Schiller, Willy Brandt, Edward Heath, the current opera season and the world currency situation. While she talked she prepared a meal for eight ravenous Victorians (who didn't turn up), produced far too many bottles of wine from a cupboard in the guest room (she'd been keeping them there in case someone got thirsty overnight) and broke it to me gently that my husband would only have a choice of four desserts. Going back to our hotel in the car, I felt horribly like a First Year who's been trying to keep up with a Fifth Former.

Even the television programmes were far more biassed towards information, discussion and documentary reports than in England, and some Germans I met were frankly culture-mad. A shoemaker's wife sat down with me and talked enthusiastically about Chaucer for hour after hour, undoubtedly imagining I must be at least as riveted by the subject as she was, and leaving me with the disquieting reflection that all I could have said to her about Goethe would have taken two minutes to utter.

Despite the time taken off for social life and observation, by the end of my visit we had eliminated so many houses and flats that no one felt slighted or left out. I was told that I was seeing the area at the worst time of year and, being convinced I was coming down with hypothermia, I felt bound to agree.

Some very peculiar things had been happening to me, which were surely not attributable to the rural Saxon nature of my temporary environment. For instance, I was ravenously hungry, especially in the mornings, and although I felt the cold terribly, hot rooms made my head swim. My queasy stomach was queasier than usual and my frontage was on an upswing. When I began fainting all over the place, with no regard for etiquette or company, my husband quizzed me about the availability of the Scarlet Pimpernel, and became very cross and patronising.

'There you are, it's obvious,' he said. 'Morning sickness . . .'

'I'm not sick in the morning, I'm starving!' I yelped.

'Not a sign of . . .'

'I'm irregular!'

'And fainting all the time. I'll rupture myself, picking you up.'

To this I had no handy retort, and it did worry me. I consulted a doctor who muttered about low blood pressure and gave me a box of tablets with terrifyingly long words on, only some of which I could interpret. He also told me to go and see my own doctor as soon as I got back to London.

'Circulatory disorder,' translated a friend with a medical dictionary, peering at my little box. 'What the Hell is wrong with you?'

'She's expecting a hypochondriac,' said my husband bitterly.

Chapter Twenty

My doctor took his head out of his hands and looked interested. The poor man gets this wild, defensive expression on his face when I walk in, but sometimes I'm worth all the trouble for my rarity value, and obviously this was one of those occasions.

'Well, well,' he said happily. 'It sounds as though you're making too much insulin. I know just the man to have a look at you.'

'What's he like?' I asked eagerly (my G.P. has come up with some real smashers over the years).

'Short and tired,' he replied. 'But good at his job.'

'Hadn't I better have a pregnancy test?' I persisted. 'If only to put my husband out of his misery?'

The doctor glanced up from the letter he was writing. 'I can't do that with a pregnancy test,' he said nastily. 'How about a divorce?'

The test was negative, but the funny symptoms hung around and the dear little specialist (who wasn't tired at all) was very intrigued. I was asked to come into hospital for some tests.

'What sort of tests?' I wanted to know, gathering up my blanket.

'Oh, just overnight. A few . . .' and he was interrupted by some students, and disappeared. So it was an ignorant and curious me who presented herself at the Reception Desk a couple of months later. The hospital wheels had ground slow, I'd been backwards and forwards to Germany so often I didn't bother to cheat the Customs any more, and my husband had assumed all the mystery, romance and inconvenience of a week-end cottage. I'd found that if I kept eating I didn't faint, so I was expensive but conscious most of the time.

The snooty girl who handled my file with her gloves on told me that there'd been a lot of 'flu cases and I'd have to be put in the Emergency Ward.

'You won't get much sleep *there*,' she said, smiling like a shark. 'Nocturnal admissions, you know!' She may have been frank about the nocturnal admissions, but she didn't tell me the ward was co-ed.

When I put my lenses back in, I realised the men were nothing to get excited about. There was one under seventy, and he looked fantastic from the neck up, but as all the rest of him was in bandages and splints he wasn't much use to me. I wasn't the only woman in the ward, but I was the only one of child-bearing age, and an octogenarian perked up enormously when I was shown the bed next to him.

'What you in for?' he mumbled, hurriedly ramming his false teeth into his mouth.

'Tests,' I said vaguely, looking round for somewhere to dump my clothes. 'You?'

Oh, how I wish I hadn't asked. Do *you* know what it's like to have your water drawn off by hand? I didn't, but I do now, much to my regret. The cheerful lady with the tea trolley was quite worried about me.

'You look ever so white,' she said. 'Want something to drink?'

I was about to croak out my usual mid-morning request for three cups of coffee when a nurse swooped on me with a notice in her hand.

'Nothing for you,' she shrilled. 'Nothing to eat or drink today. Doctor'll be along to take a blood test in a minute.' And she rushed away, leaving the notice which said 'Nil Orally' hanging on the foot of my bed. The tea lady gave me a pitying smile and moved on, and I fumbled under the bed for my slippers and went after the nurse.

'Look,' I said anxiously, 'there must be some mistake. I'm hungry all the time. I come over odd if I don't eat. I've never eaten so much as I have over the past few months. The one thing I can't do without . . .'

'Nothing,' she said briskly. 'Perhaps some water, later on. We want to find out what happens to you when you go without food.'

'Can't you take my word for it?' I wailed, but she just laughed. In a previous existence she probably sat under guillotines, knitting. I went back to bed and watched the other occupants of the ward tucking in to tea, coffee, marmite and other wholesome libations. The attractive chap winked at me over his cast but I felt only a temporary boost, and the octogenarian took his teeth out again and examined them minutely.

My neighbour on the other side was a lady of such extreme age that she would have made Lazarus look like a premature baby. She was completely deaf, very spry, and had no appetite, and as I sat through lunch (a beautiful three course meal, for those who were having it) watching a patient orderly trying to persuade her to take a bite or two, an unreasoning hatred and jealousy rose up in me like bile. I wasn't in a good mood when a young and spotty doctor came to deprive me of my much-needed blood.

'How long is this going on?' I demanded, rubbing my sore arm. 'I really am starving.'

'As long as it takes,' he replied laconically. 'I'll use a smaller needle next time. See you in two hours. 'Bye.'

The dreadful day droned on. I felt so dizzy I couldn't read, but I started a letter to my husband that was so pitiful I burst into tears before I could finish it. Energetic nurses came and went and did things to the people around me, and the little man on one side of me kept me apprised of the state of his water, and the little old lady on the other side wanted to know if I was being denied food because I hadn't got all my stamps on my card.

'That your doctor?' she enquired, pointing at the 'Nil

Orally' sign. Weakly I shook my head, but she thought I was a bit simple. 'Sadist that Orally,' I heard her mutter.

By the early evening my veins were slowly and inexorably collapsing and the marks on my right arm were enough to have me run in in Piccadilly any night of the week.

'Please,' I croaked, 'please, when can I have something to eat?'

'Ask the doctor next time he comes,' said a nurse. 'Perhaps you can have some supper.'

But the young doctor grinned fiendishly as he probed around for a still-extant vein, and said that sometimes these tests took seventy-two hours to complete. He carried away more of my blood supply and I tried to compose mentally a searing article on legalised vampirism in our hospitals today, but my concentration was shot to hell.

The other occupants of the ward began waking up (proving a theory of mine that the majority of human beings are nocturnal) and waving at one-another, and the bandaged man tried to wave at me, but a nurse reprimanded him and adjusted his splints so he couldn't move an inch. Abruptly, from somewhere off to my left, there was a quite unmistakable, and very loud, noise. I felt myself blushing all over, like at the Customs when they ask whether you've got anything to declare and you feel guilty even if you haven't. Then it happened again, exremely long-drawn-out and mournful this time, like a lonely fog-horn. Nurses bustled round the ward, patients sipped orange juice and read thrillers. No one took the slightest notice. I tried to think of my vampirism article and pretended not to see that my neighbour was attempting to draw my attention to what the nurse was doing with a bottle.

'. . . water . . .' floated vaguely towards me.

Suddenly, from the right hand side of the ward, there came a small artillery barrage. I sat bolt upright in bed. Still no one was taking any notice. I felt like the only sane man in a lunatic asylum. Now from the end of the ward came a cheerful little pop-pop-pop.

'My God!' I thought. 'They're having a competition.'

The fog-horn sounded, the artillery barrage sent ricochets round the ward and the pop-pop-popper contented himself with the minor but necessary role of descant. I crawled out to phone a friend from the public booth on the landing.

'A mixed ward!' she exclaimed. 'How fabulous for you. Are you going to sleep in your eyelashes?' I was so infuriated I slammed down the receiver. Honestly, I do have the most confoundedly stupid friends. I saw a sign to a T.V. room and promised myself I'd get there later if I had to wheel myself on a trolley, but in the meantime my appointment with fear had come round again.

'Do you like your work?' I snarled at the doctor. I had long since given up trying to flirt with him, and I have to be on the edge of the grave to lose my interest in medical men as sex objects.

'Now, now,' he soothed, bending up my elbow over a soggy bit of cotton wool. 'Tetchy!'

When I could get up, I dragged myself off to the T.V., and finding that I was offered an inspiring choice of programmes on euthanasia and acupuncture by the serious faction, I opted for bromide and was driven to a suicidal pitch by advertisements for biscuits that crunched, breakfast food that built you up, sweets you could eat between meals and pies that disembowelled themselves to reveal large chunks of fillet steak. When I started fancying the dog food I thought I'd better get back to bed.

At half past eleven I fumbled my way to the ward, which was foetid with the efforts of the competitors and in darkness except for the narrow beam of light over the night sister's desk. 'So there you are!' she hissed. 'Get into bed, you must be feeling awfully faint by now.' If looks can speak volumes, I gave her the Encyclopaedia Britannica. Opening a bottle of cologne, I shook it all over myself, my nightdress and the pillows. I was thinking

how awful it was to feel so morning-after-the-night-before when there hadn't been a night before when from the bed next door but one came what sounded like a loud sigh. Last time the lights were on, that bed had been occupied by an extremely chic old lady in a rose pink bedjacket, who'd kept herself to herself with such tenacity that the nurses had a hard time getting her blood pressure.

'Poor old thing,' I thought. 'She must be unhappy.'

The noise was repeated, louder. It wasn't a sigh after all. With nightfall any remaining inhibitions had been cast to the winds.

Half way through the gusty night, with crashings and bangings and rattles, there was one of the receptionist's nocturnal admissions. The curtains were drawn round the patient's bed and a doctor began a muttered interrogation. It took less than two minutes for this illusion of privacy to be dispelled.

'I can't 'ear yuh!' bellowed a parade ground voice. 'Speak up!'

'I said,' came a strangulated public school accent, 'do you have trouble passing water?'

'Passing *what?*' roared the patient, clearly free from laryngitis.

'Do you have bladder trouble?' the doctor screamed back. 'When you want to *go*, can you?'

'Can I *go?*' responded the scandalised R.S.M. 'What sort of question is that?'

The entire ward was awake by this time, except for the deaf lady beside me, and she missed out on a guided tour of the new man's organs. One by one and two by two, we went through everything and what it should be doing and wasn't, and what it could be doing, and hadn't. The patient was apparently disgusted by the intimacy of the examination, and spat profusely, missing the doctor but not his stethoscope or the linoleum.

'Don't spit on the floor!' cried an enraged nurse, mopping madly.

'Don't *what?*' roared the admission. 'What do you think I am, missie? And language like that from a girl!'

The rest of us broke up, and there was an appreciative salvo from the artillery section, but the nursing staff got their own back by washing the new man from head to foot and (judging by his shrieks) using a nail brush on his private parts. Seeing me wide awake after the latest blood-letting, one of the girls came over and asked for a splash of my cologne.

'The *smell*,' she whispered. 'I don't think his toenails have been cut since D-Day.'

'Here,' called her companion, from the other end of the ward. 'I've found the air freshener, thank God.' And with great ceremony they circled the curtained bed, making shadows like dancing elephants, their movements weird and ghostly in the light from the desk, the hiss of the aerosol like a charmer's snake. When they'd used up the tin they had a cup of coffee, and I'd have given anything in the world to join them.

Long before dawn we were officially roused by the distribution of bed-pans, and a more dreadful way to be woken up I cannot imagine. Not that I'd been asleep.

'Still not fed you?' shouted the elderly lady beside me, sipping at her tea. 'It's a warning not to cheat the National Health.' Then, moved by my envious glances at her cup: 'Here, have some of mine, dear.'

Unfortunately, being so deaf she wasn't able to judge how loudly she was speaking, and a watchful sister dived at us before I could take a mouthful. The doctor arrived and annexed yet more blood, but a deathly lassitude was upon me and I didn't even complain when he made four stabs at finding a vein.

'The specialist will be along before lunch,' he said nervously (I was uncannily quiet). 'And he'll probably say when you can eat.'

My stomach moaned. All around me breakfasts were being served and the sight of the volume being put away roused me from my lethargy; I had to get away from that food, it was driving me crazy. The bathroom seemed as good a refuge as any, but I'd hardly settled before there was a pounding on the door and an infant probationer wanted to know whether I was all right.

'You're not supposed to go anywhere alone,' she fussed. 'You may faint.'

I gripped the edge of the washbasin and wondered if it would be possible to tear the thing out of the wall with one's bare hands, given the strength of desperation. 'Go away,' I called, with incredible restraint. 'I am just having a wash.' But she waited outside until I reappeared and then insisted on helping me back to the ward. Considering I might as well take some advantage of the situation, I said I felt weak and must lie down on the nearest bed, which happened to belong to the bandaged young man. We were getting acquainted when my deaf neighbour came up and thumped on the bedrail, doing frightful harm to the arrangement of the pulleys.

'It's disgusting,' she shouted, shaming me into climbing down off the bed. 'Whatever she's done, they shouldn't starve her.' I got back on again. 'You are English, aren't you?' I nodded. 'There you are. If she was a Pakistani they'd feed her.'

'I wish I'd known that,' I sighed. 'I'd have blacked up before I came in.'

At noon the specialist entered and looked around for me. I could understand his difficulty; I was almost transparent. 'Ah, there you are,' he said. 'Well, you're due for another blood test in a minute and then I think we'll let you eat something, and you can go home in the afternoon.'

'Go home?' I cried. 'But what happens now? What have you found out? What's wrong with me?'

The specialist shifted from foot to foot and sucked his biro. 'Have you noticed any lessening of these fainting fits lately?' he asked.

'Yes,' I replied. 'I told my G.P. When I eat I feel miles better.'

'Um, exactly,' he said. 'Yes, well, you've worked out your own treatment, d'you see? Food little and often. You're one of those people whose blood sugar level tends to drop a bit sharply but all you have to do is nibble something and it goes up again. Keep a packet of biscuits handy. There's nothing radically wrong with you, the tests were fine.'

'Fine?' I squeaked. 'FINE! You mean it was as simple as that, and I've cured myself, and I don't need any treatment?'

'That's right,' said the specialist, backing down the ward. 'But you're reassured now, aren't you?'

'REASSURED!' I howled. 'I went through all this for nothing? Eighteen blood tests and starvation and nocturnal admissions and wind?'

'Yes, well, we don't get many patients undergoing these tests,' he muttered. 'Not many people are willing . . . I mean . . . When I was a student I volunteered . . .'

Those nurses knew what they were doing when they took the bed-pans away before the specialist came round. If I'd had a receptable handy I swear I'd have got him, but being unarmed I simply sat in bed cursing while a tray was loaded up with all the breakfast left-overs that could be found, and then I ate the lot and got up.

'Don't you want to wait?' asked the sister. 'Doctor said you should have at least two meals before you try to leave. He thought you'd be too weak to walk.'

'Let me out of here,' I spat. 'I'm getting dressed and going home.'

The splinted man waved goodbye with his eyelashes and the deaf lady, who'd sat in astonished silence while I devoured the trayload of food, said Mr Orally must be a good sort after all. As I staggered down the stairs and out through the packed entrance hall of the hospital, I wished for the millionth time that winter that some form of transport was waiting for me.

Chapter Twenty-One

High on the list of things I wasn't getting regularly from my husband were lifts in his car, and it was a service I missed very much, especially when I was incapacitated or it was raining.

'Learn to drive!' he said unhelpfully, during one of our long and exorbitant telephone conversations, but I made allowances for celibacy having impaired the functioning of his brain.

Such is my breakers' yard aura that I only have to walk past a car and it cringes and tries to hide itself under a parking ticket. Rolls-Royces puff out their radiators and look brazen because they know I can't afford them, but Minis and Fiats go pale and slip through gratings. About five years ago, when I took some driving lessons from a calm non-smoker who subsequently fell victim to nicotine poisoning and hypertension, I was known and dreaded by every vehicle in the Marylebone and St John's Wood areas where I practised my fearful circumnavigations, and dogs and cyclists got up on to the pavements when they saw me coming (not that they were any safer there).

Being travel sick didn't help much, either, because if I did something frightful and had to brake sharply, and the instructor climbed back into the passenger seat and began telling me off, almost inevitably I'd open my door and throw up. It put my tutor off his stroke completely, because he couldn't very well go on screaming at me when he was holding my head over the gutter, and after a few weeks of being seen around St John's Wood either as a blur (because once I've got into top gear I don't know how to change back down again) or the constant companion of a woman who spent her time craning out of cars being sick, he said his reputation wouldn't stand any more of it.

So I sort of promised not to try and drive, and admitted I'd known all along that I suffer from a total lack of co-ordination between my hands and feet and brain, as anybody who's ever danced with me can corroborate.

Being immobile didn't worry me when I was single, because I wouldn't have been able to park a car in Soho anyway, and when I got married chauffeuring services were part of the deal (except during the gentian violet stage), but now I had to fall back on taxis again, after a long leave. Luckily, I adore cabs; they amount to a mania with me, and I'm prepared to overlook any and all of their disadvantages. I know they don't like getting their tyres wet and go into hiding when it rains, and weld themselves in clots to Hyde Park Corner and Regent Street at five o'clock every evening, and need an emetic to regurgitate change for a note, but they've got character, which is more than you can say for a lot of private cars. And besides, don't you think it's rather exciting to get into a dark vehicle with a strange man driving and exchange opinions on all sorts of intimate topics for twenty minutes or half an hour? When you consider that you're being transported somewhere at the same time it seems an even more incredible bargain. It's cheaper than psychoanalysis and less humbling than the confessional, and feeling that I need have no conscience about the number of taxis I took because I was forced to it by lack of a husband, it was a horrible shock to me when I noticed that there weren't so many of my fantasy objects in the streets any more, and whenever I did manage to find a taxi I'd hear a heart-rending story from its driver.

'Fumes!' choked a burly chap, taking me and my packet of biscuits to Petty France. 'Bloody fumes!' He cleared out his pleural cavity and sat watching a van as it commenced unloading in front of us. 'I got stuck in an underpass for half an hour last week and nobody but me turned his bloody engine off.' He dredged around his thorax and rolled a cigarette. 'Took me two and a half hours to get from Fenchurch Street to Camden Town, and I'm not a fit man.'

I could hear he wasn't.

'I wouldn't care, but this isn't even my own cab I'm being killed in,' he crooped, 'I'm running it for a friend of mine who's unwell.'

I thought unwell was what the girls at school used to be once a month when there were hockey matches, but I kept quiet.

'We're all being poisoned,' the cabbie husked. 'There's not a driver won't tell you the same. We're all packing it in. Fumes and jams, that's all it is nowadays. Fumes and jams. Three fares an afternoon if you're lucky, and as for that Oxford Street scheme...' He actually ground into gear but it was only a display of passion; we didn't move forward, the van was still unloading. Sympathy from me resulted in the brandishing of a phial of bright yellow tablets. 'I've been put on antibiotics,' wheezed the sufferer. 'Fumes!'

'That's funny,' I said innocently. 'They look just like the diuretic pills my doctor gives me for fluid retention.'

'Christ!' whooped the driver. 'So that explains it!' And with his promises to eviscerate and geld his doctor burning in my ears we shot forward and round the van so fast we left its wing mirrors flapping in our slip-stream.

I could see that a cabbie with bladder trouble must be a worried man. Only the day before, a chatty driver had told me he'd dived down a lavatory and come panting up the steps again just two minutes later to find his cab had been towed away. He'd flagged down a friend and they'd roared off to the car pound, arriving well ahead of the police.

'But they didn't like it when they saw me there waiting for 'em and they nicked me on the spot,' he'd sighed. 'I'm chucking it in next week. I can't afford the fines.'

As every taxi driver I spoke to was either driving his cab for the last time or looked as though he should be, I became more and more depressed; what would London be like when they'd gone, and how on earth would I manage without cabbies? You get to know a man amazingly well when you've spent half an afternoon with him in a traffic jam. I've always said I'd never have married my husband if my pet psychometrist had thought it important to tell me what he was like driving to work in the mornings – he beats his head against the windscreen at red lights.

In the relatively untroubled days before I met the windscreen thumper, I went out with a very nice taxi driver, but despite the gratifying number of one-up-manship points I scored by stepping out of offices, flats and air terminals into an omnipresent cab, the relationship was brief. Well, have you ever tried parking a taxi?

One evening we went to a concert with some friends I hadn't seen for ages, and my mate soon made himself unpopular for rows around by getting up every ten minutes and shuffling out to make sure his vehicle was still there. I got fed up with apologising for him against heavy competition from Stravinsky, and after the fifth excursion my soon-to-be-ex girl friend leaned across the empty seat separating us and asked hopefully if he was ill.

'No,' I whispered self-consciously, 'he's gone to have a look at his cab.'

'His SCAB?' she shrieked, giving the brass section a run for their money. 'Did you say he's gone to have a look at his *scab*?'

'There you are, Minnie,' came an excited voice from the seat behind me. 'It was never like this in Boston.'

'His CAB,' I bellowed into an unexpected patch of pianissimo. 'His TAXI cab.'

My friend lurched back into her own seat, my cab driver shuffled in and sat down, and waves of East Coast disappointment slapped the back of my neck.

Not that all cabbies are misunderstood little angels.

When I get into a taxi I immediately look for the mirror. There isn't supposed to be an interior rear-view mirror, but there usually is, and it's interesting to see the changing expressions on the driver's face – agony, contempt, aggression, resignation – as the policemen do the sabre dance and the stew of traffic slurps. I entered a cab one afternoon and although I could see the mirror clearly, I couldn't find the driver's face in it. All the way along Knightsbridge I sat puzzling and squirming around on the back seat, but no matter what I did I couldn't see a face in the mirror, not even my own. Then a week later, it happened again. This time I was determined not to be thwarted, and explored every possible position that I could achieve with any decency and my ligaments intact, but it wasn't until I was crouching on the floor of the cab with my head resting against the seat that I could find the reflection I was looking for. Just what was visible at that angle?

'Oh!' I said, going pink with inspiration, and I got up off the floor and sat very straight, my knees clamped together, as we crawled round the Aldwych. When I scrambled out the young cabbie flipped through his money and commented that he remembered me.

'Took you to the Linquists Club last week, didn't I? Lovely pair of legs you've got.'

'You should know,' I snapped, marching off before he could say how much he liked my underwear, but I hadn't gone far before I started grinning and feeling flattered. When you think how many legs he must have seen! The only trouble with this sort of complimentary behaviour is that cabbies can also be possessive about their fares. I was sitting in a taxi at some traffic lights when I glanced out of the window and straight into the gorgeous face of a driver who'd drawn up alongside. He smiled at me, I smiled at him, and we were enjoying ourselves enormously when my cab-driver shot the lights and nearly broke my neck getting away up Portland Place.

'What was that for?' I shouted, picking myself up and

checking that nothing vital was broken or detached. Could I perhaps sue him for the loss of a contact lens?

'I saw you!' roared the assassin. 'I saw you smiling at him! When you're in *my* cab you smile at *me*, understand?'

'Yes, sir,' I stammered. Really, the sooner I was back with my husband the better. He'd never get into a jealous snit over a silly little thing like that.

Chapter Twenty-Two

Or at least I thought he wouldn't. I meant so well when I sent him the photograph; it was sentimental of me, but I thought he could put it on his desk and imagine it was nagging him. I wasn't prepared for the telephone call that came through from Germany like a crossbow bolt.

'Exactly what,' came a well known voice down the wire, a voice straining through set teeth, 'did you have on when this picture was taken?'

'Well, er, the photographer wanted to create a romantic effect, as though I had an evening dress on, but I didn't have anything like that with me so we had to improvise.'

'Where are the straps?'

'Straps?'

'Your bra straps. Where are they? You don't wear strapless bras. You *can't* wear strapless bras. From this photograph it looks as if . . .'

Sherlock bloody Holmes, I groaned. He couldn't tell you whether I got married in black or white, but he knows more about my underwear than I do. And it seemed such a harmless idea at the time. I'd gone to a West End studio in slacks and a blouse to have a casual photograph taken to send to my husband, and before I knew what was happening I'd signed enough official documents to keep a department of the internal revenue happy for a week and had been thrust into a cubicle and told to take off as many clothes as I wanted. It was cold outside and nobody attractive was hanging around so I didn't want to take any clothes off, but I combed my hair and came out again.

The studio looked like a garage, with aluminium foil stretched over a large section of the floor and running up the wall at one end, and a keen photographer and some very hot arc lights planted in the middle. I sat on a stool in the centre of the foil and immediately started to cook. After ten minutes I'd undone my blouse to the navel and sweat was trickling into my eyes. Ten minutes more and when the photographer suggested I should take my blouse off and drape a scarf round my shoulders I asked if he could run the scarf under a cold tap first.

'And this had better go, it shows,' he said purposefully, undoing a clip and whipping away my bra. I couldn't have cared less. Sweat was pouring down my arms and plopping off my elbows on to the foil, where it turned to stream. Hours went by and I thought of ice cubes and frozen lakes and skating rinks, and then it was all over and I got dressed, went out into foggy London and caught a stinking cold. Of the rather startling prints from which I eventually had to choose, I selected the least revealing and sent it off to my husband, and this was what I was getting for my pains.

'If you expect me to keep this on my desk at the office you must be even madder than you used to be,' he was bawling. 'The post boy who opened it has already come and said "Iss your vife an egzotik danzer?" And what's all this about your dentist hypnotising you to unclench your psyche, and those cosy little sessions with your masseur?'

'But in your last letter you said you wanted me to write and tell you *all* my news,' I protested. 'You said it would make you feel as though I was there yattering at you in person if I put the trivial detail in as well.'

'Trivial detail!' There was heavy breathing at the other end of the line. 'I feel like someone out of *Brief Encounter*,' he said finally. 'Which would be more fun if I weren't married to you. This long-distance commuting has got to stop. Whatever the next house looks like, I'm taking it, and *you* are coming over here. Permanently. No more hypnotism, no more masseurs, nothing.' He sounded quite frighteningly masterful and teutonic, like a Chartered Accountant who's managed to create a loss.

'Oh, dear,' I sighed, putting down the phone. 'How am I going to explain to everybody?'

The dentist took it like a man. He quite saw that all those hours of relaxing a joint at a time and concentrating on balloons would have to end, but he insisted I continue to care for my teeth, and gave me a packet of Inter-dens as a parting present. The masseur was less reasonable and kept asking querulously what was going to happen to my muscle tone, and my hairdresser had to be revived with the kiss of life.

'On your own head be it,' he said grimly, and if I got my dandruff back I couldn't blame him, and he was unable to recommend anyone to cut my hair north of Stuttgart.

'They still paint themselves with woad, north of Stuttgart,' he said bitterly.

Although the professionals in my life took my departure seriously, the news that my husband had indeed found a house and was having our furniture brought out of store threw my friends into a state of unparalleled lethargy.

'But I'm going in two weeks,' I told them.

'Oh, yeah?' was the most convinced reply.

It seemed that having been through numerous false alarms with me, they were impervious to the drama of the situation. My husband had found houses before, they said, and I'd gone and seen them, hadn't I? There was the fairytale one with a beautiful cherry tree in the garden and six feet of stagnant water in the cellar. And there was the fantastic modern flat with everything you could possibly wish for, and some things you couldn't, like the barbed wire and being so handy for Belsen. And there'd been the dream-home that slept fifteen without compromising anybody and we only found out when our pens were poised to sign that the Eurodot was in the wrong place and it wasn't a bargain after all.

'Come, come,' said my friends 'what do you take us for?'

'Friends!' I said. 'Who will help me with the luggage.'

As I was being telephoned hourly with instructions regarding what I should bring with me, the luggage was not a light matter. My husband's last request for Boots razor blades had evoked an outburst of trans-Continental temper from me.

'There's no room,' I'd stormed. 'As it is I'll have to leave my dildo behind.'

My mother's flat was unrecognisable under a three-feet-deep layer of clothing, books and going-away presents which had accumulated during the preceding months, every call I had that wasn't from Lower Saxony was an invitation to something heavenly taking place after I'd gone, and people who'd hardly noticed me before were struck with compassion and took me out for drinks. The date of my flight got moved back a week.

'I haven't had my tax repayment yet,' I explained to my husband (rather cannily, I thought), 'and I've got to hand in my National Insurance Card.'

'I suppose it's just as well,' he said grudgingly, 'because I'm going to Vienna anyway.'

He was flitting around Europe like a bowler-hatted wasp and I had every intention of accompanying him in the future.

'I've never seen Vienna,' I told him.

'You will,' he said, and hung up. Then he rang back, sounding nervous. 'I was wondering what you'd like as a welcome present,' he gulped.

That is the question for which I am always prepared in case the opportunity doesn't arise again, so I rattled off about sixteen items and left him to mop his brow and find some hard currency. It would be nice to give *him* a present, I thought, and what would be useful, and romantic, and something he'd appreciate?

In circumstances such as this, a girl's gynaecologist can be her best friend. I went to see mine for a final check-up before flying off to the frozen wastes.

'Did you know,' he said idly, 'That there's a new kind of I.U.D. specially suitable for women who haven't had kids? Tiny little thing, it is, but 98 per cent successful.'

'Tell me more,' I urged, a few rusty cogs winding on in my brain and my husband's detestation of Wellington Boots vivid in my mind.

'There's a pamphlet here, read all about it,' said the doctor. 'Plastic holding virgin copper, but not for long! Hoh, hoh, hoh!' (My gynaecologist has a sense of humour; he *has* to have.)

'Do you think it might be good for my rheumatism too?' I asked, but he wasn't sure about that. He explained it very carefully, however, and a few days later fitted it so painlessly that I didn't know he'd done it, and showed me how to check it was still in place, and said he thought it was a lovely idea for a present.

I felt so liberated, walking about impregnable like that. Nothing to take, nothing to do, and my husband waiting for me in Germany like a Christmas stocking all ready to be emptied out on the bed. The chaos of departure only added to my mounting excitement. No best man and no thrush this time; I promised myself a whole new beginning.

So I rushed from shops to social security offices and from insurance companies to banks, and in between I went to see films and plays and old friends, and made outrageous avowals to those I didn't think I'd be seeing for years, and promised to write to everybody. Overtiredness gave me hallucinations but it also blunted the shock of leaving my mother and aunt in Soho with the latest intake of pneumatic drills, demolition squads and 'save our historic buildings' campaigners.

During my last twenty-four hours in London I found it hard to be sensible and unsentimental, and after a sleepless night of tranquillisers that wouldn't work I began cheering myself up with alcohol far too soon. As a result I was so anaesthetised and chummy that when the girl on the Lufthansa cash desk told me I was £21.96 overweight

I just smiled and drew a cheque on our vanquished joint account.

The crew on the flight to Hanover thought I was stoned until they saw the members of the British Trade Mission weaving up the aisle behind me, blue flames dancing on their breath. I filled up the seat next to me with hand baggage and acquired a prim Westphalian lady as a fielder, but these tank traps were easily avoided by a roguish gent one row back who talked at me loudly and pinched me hard through the more penetrable sections of the seat when I ignored him.

'Hey, Blondie! Have a drink?' and 'Hey, Blondie! I'll break my neck if I go on talking round the back of your chair like this!' came plaintively from behind my head, as the plane broiled through the blue above the cloudly weather, and the stewards smiled at me sympathetically and suggested that the gentlemen in that section should keep their seat belts fastened. When we put down at Bremen my hair was permeated with the smell of gin and the Westphalian lady pointedly changed her seat. I'd learned that my tired, tipsy and now wasp-waisted admirer was promoting Irish butter and hoped to marry a fair haired girl about six feet tall who didn't speak to strange men, but he disembarked with the rest of the Trade Mission and I took the ham out of my Lufthansa snack and chewed it stoically as we flew on to Hanover. I fell down the aeroplane steps when I got there, just as I'd done the first time, and was still dusting myself off in the car when my husband gave me a small, smart box with a jeweller's name on it and sat back looking expectant.

'Well?' he said.

'Well what?'

'Where's *my* present?'

'I was wearing it,' I said uneasily,' but I fell down those steps again and now I'm not too sure.'

He didn't speak to me for five hours.

Whatever our life in Lower Saxony is like, I have a feeling you'll find out.

ALIDA BAXTER

FLAT ON MY BACK
UP TO MY NECK
OUT ON MY EAR

The hilarious saga in which Alida Baxter gets to the root of what living and loving in the '70s is all about – entirely dismembering her husband, sex and marriage . . .

'The funniest books I've read for years.' GOOD HOUSE-KEEPING

'In the long line of a writing tradition that includes Richard (Doctor in the House) Gordon, and James (Let Sleeping Vets Lie) Herriot . . . wholly worthwhile entertainers.' SMITH'S TRADE NEWS

'Ms. Baxter does a most difficult thing very well. She makes her life not only funny but interesting.' DAILY MIRROR

'Her honeymoon, a move to Germany, in-laws, out-laws – Alida treats them all like a slide on a banana skin. The result is just as hilarious.' ANNABEL

'Hilariously funny.' OVER 21

'Happily recommended.' FORUM

'Smiles all the way.' BOOKS AND BOOKMEN

THE ORIGINAL BESTSELLING VET BOOKS

by

Alex Duncan

IT'S A VET'S LIFE
THE VET HAS NINE LIVES
VETS IN THE BELFRY

A true and outrageously funny series concerning the exploits of veterinary surgeon Michael Morton, the animals in his care, and the owners the animals really owned.

'What Richard Gordon has done for doctors, Alex Duncan is doing for vets.' BOOKS AND BOOKMEN

'The author's fast and furious pace never conceals a hard core of veterinary experience.' THE COUNTRYMAN

'See how the Richard Gordon formula works just as successfully with animals.' PHILIP OAKES

'*Vets in the Belfry* is like its predecessors – or even more so – very funny indeed.' CATHOLIC HERALD

'Alex Duncan looks like becoming the Richard Gordon of the animal clinics.' LONDON EVENING NEWS

THE MARX BROS. SCRAPBOOK

Groucho Marx and Richard J. Anobile

'Virtually all the beans are spilled . . . What rich and fascinating material it is.' NEW YORK MAGAZINE

'The best record of the family's life . . . uninhibited not to say earthy when Groucho lets the language rip.' DAILY MIRROR

'A treasure-trove for Marx Brothers fans and for movie-goers generally . . . This is a remarkable book, a funny book, and one to read through again and again.' WHAT'S ON

'The all-time definitive work on the subject. A collector's item . . . A classic.' CHICAGO SUN-TIMES

'No true Marx Brothers buff will be without it.' YORKSHIRE POST

'Compelling gossip.' THE TIMES

'Hugely enjoyable . . . It's especially good to see Groucho at 83 in such candid and caustic form.' OXFORD MAIL

This is the controversial, 'scandalous', beguiling and absolutely authentic memoir of the most famous foursome in movie history, recounted by none other than the master himself. With 300 splendid illustrations and memorabilia to bring you for the first time, *the one, the only, the real Marx Bros.*

75p

Wyndham Books are obtainable from many booksellers and newsagents. If you have any difficulty please send purchase price plus postage on the scale below to:

Wyndham Cash Sales,
123 King Street,
London W6 9JG

OR

Star Book Service,
G.P.O. Box 29,
Douglas,
Isle of Man,
British Isles

While every effort is made to keep prices low, it is sometimes necessary to increase prices at short notice. Wyndham Books reserve the right to show new retail prices on covers which may differ from those advertised in the text or elsewhere.

U.K. & Eire
One book 15p plus 7p per copy for each additional book ordered to a maximum charge of 57p.

Other Countries
Rates available on request.

These charges are subject to Post Office charge fluctuations.